Shane Kind was born and raised in the north of England and spent many years travelling around the country before finally settling in Cambridge, UK.

To my family, who patiently put up with my constant ramblings, to Diane, Emma and Hannah.

Shane Kind

THE SHATTERED REALMS
BOOK 1: THE GREAT ARMY

AUSTIN MACAULEY PUBLISHERS™

LONDON • CAMBRIDGE • NEW YORK • SHARJAH

A CIP catalogue record for this title is available from the British Library.

ISBN 9781398479067 (Paperback)
ISBN 9781398479074 (ePub e-book)

www.austinmacauley.com

First Published 2023
Austin Macauley Publishers Ltd®
1 Canada Square
Canary Wharf
London
E14 5AA

Thank you Austin Macauley Publishers for believing in me.

Table of Contents

1 In the Beginning

The king of Mārcādiā, Eadweard se Ieldra, had invited over thirty guests to his hunting lodge in the countryside that weekend, and while all of his male guests had joined him on the hunt, their partners had stayed back at the lodge to enjoy the more tranquil of sports, like lawn croquet. The sun was high in the sky, and everyone was enjoying the warmth of a summer's day in the outdoors. The guards were milling around the outer walls but in chainmail armour, and with heavy leather tabards, it was getting hard to concentrate on their duties to guard the ladies and the prince.

As the ladies laughed and enjoyed the company of their own and the children were larking around pretending to be knights or kings, just like their fathers it was understandable that they might have all missed the first cry that sounded as the guards came under attack from persons unknown. In fact, it so happened that the second shout of a dying guard coincided exactly with the shouts of the young prince, Ēadmund, as he pretended to stab the son of the king's champion, Arathorn.

It was the king's champion's wife who first noticed that something was dreadfully wrong and it was possibly her quick thinking that saved the young eight-year-old prince's life. She called him over to her and she held tightly on to his hand and told him he must come inside the lodge, and reluctantly he did just as he was told to do, However, Lady Helena Amabilis's ten-year-old son wasn't so lucky.

The attackers killed four of the women at random and then they snatched at the ten-year-old boy who at the time was considered small for his age, because he fit the description of the young prince that they had really come to kidnap? They did not ask questions and they did not hang around for more guards than they could handle to arrive, and so one of them picked up the boy and they disappeared the way that they had come, leaving no trace other than the bodies of those four unfortunate ladies.

Mārcādiā was the richest and most powerful of all the kingdoms that made up the lands known as the Shattered Realms, and it had acquired many enemies both at home and in the countries that lay over the Dark Water Channel because of its prosperity, and some would say because of the envy of the gods. If the Shattered Realms were once considered the jewel in the worlds crown, then Mārcādiā was most certainly the diamond in its heart.

When a ransom note was passed one day to the king Ēadweard se Ieldra for a large sum of money to have his son returned, it was understandable that he took no notice of the demands and instead gave the note to one of his stewards to deal with. Prince Ēadmund had until this time been kept hidden away just in case this day arrived, and the king wanted the villains who perpetrated this heinous crime to be completely fooled.

However, the steward who was passed the note was not a supporter of the king and so he cared little for the life of his son, and in fact did quite the opposite to what he was expected to do. He burnt the note on a nearby candle and forgot that he had ever been given it. Shortly thereafter, he left the employ of the palace leaving no forwarding address, in the staunch belief that the king would suffer for all that he done to wrong the steward in the past.

Now it should be said that the Shattered Realms had become the playground of the gods ever since the one true God, Ĕlyāh, had lifted up the enchanted isle and threw it back to earth in a fit of temper at his spirit children, one in particular that had disobeyed his express wishes only to create Humanoid creates in his image, the angel, Lōthōs. That is how the isles got their name, they shattered on impact and each part became surrounded by great rivers and mountains that were impassable for many hundreds of years until just after the beginning of the second age, when a dominant race of men called the Kristosiān's came in boats to conquer the lands.

Some realms remained untamed though as they were far away to the north across rough and dangerous rivers and seas, and they were teaming with barbarian tribes of Orsk, and Northmen who would not be subjugated. Unbeknown to any though, there was a queen who through unrequited love had found a safe haven amongst one of the northern tribes and she was plotting revenge against the one who so callously broke her heart.

There was a legend that came with the Shattered Realms, and it went something like this, when all around is in disarray and the end of times is staring you in the face, then look to the scarecrow king for he will renounce such titles in favour of someone else, but he is the thread that will stitch and weave and pull them all together, the Re-United Kingdoms.

13

But what as this got to do with the ten-year-old boy in our story, perhaps nothing at all because when next he opened his eyes, he was staring into the face of a fellow captive of the Orsk. Her name was Beitris Fhionnlaidh and she was his mother and together they lived in a cave in the kingdom under the mountain and although he was free to wonder around the main chamber, she was not, instead her left ankle was shackled by a chain to the wall of her cell that was a cave that had been dug out of the sandstone rock.

Not all of the children were human, some were markedly different although the boy did not know why nor did he think to ask. They were like him in every way except that their skin was of a greyish hue and they had two teeth either side of their bottom jaw that protruded ever so slightly, but they were fun to play with if exceptionally strong for their ages. What was noticeable though was that there were no grey skinned girls, not that he had seen anyway, just boys, and come to think of it, the human girls were each taken away the day after they began to have the bleed.

By the age of eleven, he stood just a couple of inches short of five feet, his eyes were of a piercing hazel colour and his hair was mousy brown, nothing else unusual except for two small bumps one on either ear lobe that would be missed by those who didn't stare, and he found friends easily amongst the other children in the main chamber, of which there were many and part from the odd days when he was taken to do simple menial tasks for the Orsk, his days were endless days of play when he would organise the other children in to various role playing activities.

Not that anyone inside the cave system would have known it as such, but the year in the outside world was around nine hundred in the second age, which would have been written down S.A. and the end of the second age, for the Orsk that meant that much of their cohesiveness and rationale, was falling apart because the very thing that held them together, magic, or in their case, dark magic, was passing from the world and already the Orsk were a backward facing race, brutal and barbaric having only rudimentary skills, who lived in caves during the day and roamed far and wide during the night, there only allies were the lesser race of Kobold's who were nothing more than two legged rats and who lived even deeper in the earth.

Now in order for the Orsk system of things to work, they relied heavily at times on the Kobold, for it was the later who dealt with all of the Orsk garbage, one important area of garbage was when the women captives were no longer able to have children, or if they were of an age but unable to conceive, then they were given to the Kobold, in exchange the Kobold, who were extremely good miners, would provide the Orsk with all the iron ore and other precious metals they desired.

There was one other downside to life in captivity for the boy and that was on those occasions when all of the children were rounded up and taken out to large room, again that had been carved out of the surrounding sandstone, and tasked to sort out cloths and things that were just piled up in the rooms centre. It was on those evenings that the boy later learned that the Orsk would have their way with the women who were powerless to stop what was happening. Many a time, he would be returned to his mother and would finding her weeping inconsolably.

The boy grew to hate what he knew the Orsk were doing, and from that young age he vowed one day to escape and to return with an army big enough to teach these green skinned monsters a lesson they would never forget. Until that day though, he just had to knuckle down and bide his time, and at the age of twelve he was given something else to focus on.

All of the boys, who had turned twelve, were be paired up with a grey skin of the same age and together they would learn sword craft, or at least a very elementary version of it, given to them by an Orsk master, the first lesson was to know your name, the boy once had a name but it had been so many years since anyone had used it. He had forgotten what it was, but today he was given a new name by the Orsk master.

"My name is chief Snag-Roth," the Orsk said. "And I am responsible for your lives from this day forward, and if you obey my commands, then we shall all get along just fine. If on the other hand you wish to test my patients. Well then, I will introduce you to the Kobold who live deep down in the earth, and they would just love to have a tasty morsal like one of you for dinner."

Snag-Roth gave the boy the name Ro-Gan, which he said meant, 'Go far' in his native tongue, and he gave the grey skin the name On-Gar which translated to, 'Hammer blow'. Ro-Gan wanted to learn as much about the Orsk as he could and he found himself more often than not in the company of Snag-Roth, who in turn took a shine to the lad and his companion and together they would learn more about each other's language and cultures.

Ro-Gan was soon beating everyone he fenced with, as he remembered the times when he trained with his human father before he was taken captive, and he was a fast learner picking up the language of the Orsk so that he could speak it freely with the other Orsk he came across in his daily life, and as he was an affable enough boy, the other Orsk would engage with him in simple conversation, and he began to learn many of their secrets.

By the time he had reached thirteen, Ro-Gan and his troop were allowed to go outside and hunt for food. The land was baron of any trees and even in summer, it seemed very cold. It wasn't helped by the fact that all their hunting expeditions were carried out at night. Ro-Gan and On-gar learned to work as a team and before long, they were catching more of the animals they came across than any other pair of boys.

Until now, the hunts were in the local area close to the main entrance to the cave he knew as home, and the animals would all be small, mostly different small birds, for gulls lived all over the mountain that dominated the landscape in their thousands, and eggs of course they were the easiest of all to obtain, otherwise it would be brown hare, badgers, foxes, ducks, grouse and the like. Until one time Snag-Roth invited the two boys to hunt with the Orsk for bigger game, like deer, wild boar and grey wolves.

At age fourteen, Snag-Roth took the two boys out hunting the biggest prey that they had ever seen, the eight-foot brown bear, and this was where coordinated teamwork paid off, and both boys became much welcomed on the hunts away from the caves and tunnels because of their exceptional understanding and camaraderie.

It was times like these where Ro-Gan really cemented his place as head of the women's chamber with his tall tales of daring do and recalling funny stories about times when they were out hunting. One such story was how On-Gar and he were tracking a deer and trying to stay down wind of it. They were so focused on the animal that they did not see Snag-Roth as he had crept in front of Rogan just as he loosed his first arrow, and it flew low and struck the Orsk master in the rear end!

Another story he tells of was when they were taken for a trek in the forest where they came across a party of trolls out hunting for food themselves in the woods. The trolls were over eight feet tall and carried giant wooden clubs and they were so hungry that they wanted to eat the young humans and half-bloods and so a quarrel broke out between the trolls and the Orsk, and although the trolls were bigger and stronger, the Orsk outnumbered them, so a compromise had to be reached.

Rogan came up with a plan, he asked Snag-Roth which herbs of the forest were powerful enough to knock these trolls out, and Snag-Roth told him that there was a plant, when mixed with other herbs would knock out a troll. It was a recipe that the Orsk would use on a wounded comrade that was in great pain, one sip of the liquid and they were knocked clean out.

Snag-Roth gave Ro-Gan a list and a description of each, Deadly nightshade, Poison hemlock, Lōthōs' bolete, Wolfsbane and Fly agaric, but Snag-Roth warned that they were deadly to a human, and he wanted to know what he proposed to do, but Ro-Gan said that he would only speak in front of everyone including the trolls, and so Snag-Roth called for a meeting in which he allowed Ro-Gan to talk.

Rogan began by saying how impressed he had been by the trolls, and that he particularly liked their weapons. They were proper weapons and he said that he bet that the trolls were the most fearsome creatures in all the forest, and of course they agreed. In fact they were so feared that if they wanted to each just one boy each, then that should have caused so much trouble, because after all there were so many boys, surely the Orsk would not miss a couple or three.

However, if you have ever eaten a boy, then you will know that best way to cook one is to drop him headfirst in a pan of boiling water, and again the trolls agreed, but when drawing them out on exactly how many boys they had actually eaten, they looked rather embarrassed to say that they had never eaten a boy, but that they had heard that they were tasty.

Rogan said that boys were full of all the good things a troll would need to make him big and strong, and the trolls were really beginning to enjoy the company of this boy and so they said that they would pick three of the other boys to eat instead of him, and Ro-Gan said that in honour of their new found friendship he was going to teach them a little secret to do with cooking boys.

"Tell us! Tell us!" they shouted excitedly, and Ro-Gan said much better than tell them he would go off into the woods alone to find the perfect ingredients that would make the boys softer and tastier than anything they had ever eaten, and they let me go all alone to find these special ingredients. But he warned them that the water must be boiling hot by the time he came back because the herbs needed to be as fresh as they could be, so no eating the boys early.

When Ro-Gan returned with the plants that Snag-Roth had told him about, he threw them in the pot of boiling water and began to mix them together, and he said just for good measure they should add any vegetables that might have on their persons. Greedily, they turn out their pockets and produced such things as carrots and turnips and so other root vegetables that Ro-Gan didn't recognise but said that they would all be perfect.

Ro-Gan took each vegetable, sliced it up, and added it to the pan. Then after stirring it for many minutes to make the trolls impatient, he announced that the soup was ready, and that they should each chose a boy to eat, and after they had, and those boys looked at Ro-Gan wide eyed in terror, he said, "Oh pardon me but would you first like to taste the soup?"

You know that they couldn't resist so they each took a large wooden spoon from their pouches and proceeded to dip it in the soup. "Now go on eat it up and tell me it isn't the best thing you have ever tasted, in fact isn't it just to die for!" And the boys all grimaced at his poor joke but loved the story nonetheless and would from time to time ask him if it were true. And he would always say, "Go and ask Snag-Roth if you don't believe me!" And Snag-Roth would always laugh and shake his head when the boys approached him in secret to ask if it were true.

About halfway through that year, when Ro-Gan had counted four winters and one summer, the boys were taken to another area somewhere at the back of their compound. It was the hottest place on earth Ro-Gan believed because it was a large cave filled with blacksmith forges, and there were a handful of Orsk there who would teach the boys a new skill, they were to become blacksmiths.

So began the working day, armour was made, chest plates, and arm and leg grieves, helmets, shields and large swords that had one blunt edge and one serrated, weapons that those boys could barely lift off the ground let alone swing around in action, but they were told in private that these weapons and the armour was not for them to use. Although none of that mattered at such times that they felt their masters were looking elsewhere and then they would fool around pretending to be knights wielding those weapons, and if nothing else, in a relatively short space of time the boys' bodies certainly benefited from all that work.

There was another strange practice that was introduced shortly after the boys were introduced to blacksmithing, and that was the new custom each morning after they had been risen from their sleep, of having to strip down to there under garments and then proceed to wash and then shave off any noticeable hair from all over their bodies, and so there they would stand all in a row while Snag-Roth would walk up and down looking them all over, and any boy who missed shaving was beaten with a leather strap across the back.

Next came the twist. Once all the hair was removed, the boys were given buckets each that were filled with a rather obnoxious green dye with which they were then instructed to paint themselves all over with. The dye was derived from plants, so it was not actually harmful to either the humans or the half-breeds, a nick name the Orsk seemed to have started to use in conjunction with the grey skins.

*

After the icky green dye had dried, which took about as long as it did to administer, the boys would each put on brown woollen trousers and a brown woollen tunic along with a pair of soft leather boots and a belt of the same material.

The hunting trips were fewer by far these days and it seemed like as they grew up the boys were being given more task to do around the inside of the caves than they once were, and Ro-Gan wondered if other boys in other cases were taking over their old jobs, because Snag-Roth had talked about other caves and other boys.

Ro-Gan knew that where he lived was only a tiny part of a much, much bigger complex, although he only actually knew about the one, he lived in, so there were three main cave areas and a single tunnel that led to the outside world. One large cave was to the left of the tunnel and one was to the right and the third was at the end of the main tunnel. Ro-Gan lived with the other boys still in the women's chamber which was off the main tunnel just before the third cave and just after the first cave to the left, Ro-Gan and On-Gar had been allowed to move in together after Ro-Gan's mother had passes away, otherwise all the other boys seemed to be still living with their birth mothers.

Soon Ro-Gan's thoughts turned to the winter months, when the temperature outside was incredible cold and everywhere you looked it was just white with snow, back in the past this had become a time of giving and receiving gifts and although for the life of him Rogan could not remember why, he still missed being able to, whether talking to Snag-Roth about those times as a small child made an impression or not this particular year Snag-Roth rounded them all up and took them to a new cave at the end of the tunnel, beyond the blacksmith forges and the third cave where others lived.

In the centre of this new cave were piles of clothing and leather armour. Leather caps, leather arm grieves and heavy more hard-wearing leather boots. Snag-Roth said that the boys had Ro-Gan and On-Gar to thank for all this but in actuality, it was more to do with Ro-Gan's fifth year of captivity and their fifteenth. Whatever the reason, the boys went wild trying on different pieces of leather armour and asking each other how they looked.

Later that same day, Ro-Gan noticed that there were some new girls who had been brought to the women's chamber. At first, they were not chained like the others and Ro-Gan didn't understand why, he showed a genuine interest in all of the women and the new girls, not in a sycophantic way, but out of a feeling that he needed to protect them especially from the pain that Orsk inflicted upon them. The other boys mostly turned a blind eye to that sort of thing, it made it easier for them, that way.

Solveig looked sullen of the new girls. She was constantly in tears and always bitterly sad. She was a rather plain looking young girl of fourteen or fifteen years, and when she was not sobbing her heart out would tell the other girls about her days as a maid servant in the queen's castle in Råvenniå, of course nobody believed her, which consequently made her sadder, but they would still sit for hours to listen to her stories.

Halla Greilanda was probably the prettiest of the new girls and she was certainly the most popular amongst all the males, she was around fifteen when she was brought into the chambers, but she was as wild as a mountain cat, she had no idea where she had come from, and could not write a single letter never mind any words, she was also cunning as a tundra fox and she soon learnt that if she cosied up to On-Gar, most of the other boys would stick to admiring her from a distance.

Then there was Ingrid Hallgerd, the one who made it clear that she liked Ro-Gan from the outset, however, he did not see her as anything more than a sister, in fact that was pretty much how he viewed all of the girls in the chamber, and of course he saw all of the boys as his brothers. Ingrid as a result was

23

always sulking around Ro-Gan and constantly in a mood with him.

The last of the new girls was called Sigrunn Hallkatla and she saw herself as every bit the equal of any of the boys and she was constantly picking fights with them. She had skills and Ro-Gan would often spar with her because of it, she was from Råvenniå, and she had been picked up on the streets of the capital for propositioning boys, which the authorities took a dislike to.

While it seemed to lighten the mood about the place for the boys, for the girls it was the beginning of their worst nightmare. They had been brought here to be taught their new way of life, that which was to be at the beck and call of the Orsk whenever they wanted female company. They would cook, clean and generally do any menial task that the Orsk deemed befitted their station, that of a concubine.

All of the males, both human and half-blood, had been there from their birth and so they had a strong bond of brotherhood, but even at this early age they had taken a shine to Ro-Gan, he was a likeable rouge from the moment he was introduced to the chamber. He was cheeky but in a witty kind of way and he was intelligent, far more than any other boy and most of the Orsk, and even they enjoyed his company, he was eager to please, and he had a lust for information.

Of the other males in the chamber, Ro-Gan had particularly bonded with there was Gun-Nar, On-Gar, At-Li, Oi-Paz, Atru-Mir, Sorn-Usk, Dri-Gar and Bren-Mir.

These were the boys that were taken on hunting parties together and they were taught tracking skills by the older Orsk at night, there were many other boys there as well but some would rather keep their own company or they were happy to form smaller groups with each other rather than join in with Ro-Gan and his group.

The Orsk arranged wrestling tournaments for the younger boys which helped with all manner of skills and built good muscle tone, which the half-bloods, who seemed to develop quicker, always liked to show off. Ro-Gan wasn't as well built however, what he lacked in muscle tone he more than made up in agility, and he won his fair share of matches by using his wits and agility.

However, it wasn't always a lark with Rogan he was approaching a difficult time in his life with the change from boyhood to adulthood and when in the company of a father or uncle or any other adult he imagined it would be easy to talk about these changes, but he had only his mother to ask, and while she did her best because she had come to think of Rogan as her own, she still struggled to properly explain some things, especially when it involved the new girls.

Now as it transpired on one of these particular days that Rogan was struggling, his mother said she would ask Snag-Roth if she could put on a bit of a spread to cheer him up. She said that it was almost five winters since he was first brought to the chamber, and that it just so happened that it was also his birthday.

Snag-Roth had little or no idea what the women were talking about but as it was for Ro-Gan, he would see what he could do to bring a little extra food that evening, so all through the day, the women did their best to tidy the chamber and make it look nice and they made things to hang from the walls that were basic but pretty like corn dolls out of the straw from the floor and such like.

Rogan had been chosen to go out on a hunt hat night and Snag-Roth said that he could catch an extra animal for the celebratory meal.

It was while Ro-Gan and On-Gar were away on a that hunt that Ro-Gan's mother died, it was nothing that anyone had done, it was just her time, and by the time that Rogan had returned to the women's chambers, her body had been removed, just like that, and he never even got to say goodbye.

Ro-Gan's world seemed just to fall apart over night and all he ever wanted to do after that was fight, train and hunt, and that old hatred of all things Orsk, began to return with an insatiable appetite, once more he watched and he waited, listened, and learned, of all the secrets that nobody was supposed to know about ever, and became cold and calculating.

Snag-Roth did his best to coax the boy out of his deep routed grief but it was to no avail and soon even Snag-Roth found himself becoming distant with the boy, and now at every opportunity, he talked with the others in his troop and the talk was always about escape and revenge, and even some of the other humans began to get fed up listening to Ro-Gan.

On-Gar never did and in fact if it were possible those two grew even closer, On-Gar would hang off every word Ro-Gan would say in connection with his old life, much of which Ro-Gan himself could no longer remember, but he had a vivid imagination and On-Gar was hooked.

2 Coming of Age

How does one glean hope when it matters not if your eyes are open or closed, and there is no natural or artificial light to give even a glimmer of hope? When one rolls on ones back to look up at the stars and to pray to the one true God and there is nothing, no stars and no answer to those prayers.

When the winter chill begins to bite and it is all that you can do to curl tightly into a ball to keep warm, even when every muscle and sinew cries out to stretch and be free, but what is freedom when your nights are spent in chains and your days in enforced servitude.

And yet, you take another breath, and the tepid dry atmosphere causes your throat to tighten and gasp for yet more of that same filthy smelling dry air, why does life cling to one's bones when there is no useful purpose for it to do so, because, maybe, just maybe, God has not abandoned you, and today shall be the day that you rise up and bath in his almighty glory and he will deliver those who seek to devour you, into your own hands, and the Lord God say's vengeance is mine.

"Wake up, Ro-Gan. No time to have a lay in." The smell of burning oil now permeated into the nostrils, seeking to drive the smell of human waste away, and it is a welcome smell, that ushers in the start of a new day.

That morning, On-Gar was awake first and he was the one who lit the torches in the cave and in the corridor outside, the same thing was being repeated all down the corridor, in fact in hundreds of corridors that ran the length and breathe of the kingdom under the mountains.

Ro-Gan would then take the overnight bucket to the sluice pit and tip it away before swapping it for a bucket full of fresh spring water from the stream that ran down one side of the central cavern and down the corridor and out on to the moors.

Every morning, the boys woke to the same routine, strip and shave, and then paint themselves all over with a thick green dye, all the human boys and all of the half-blood boys. The dye took no more time to dry than it did to administer, once that was done, they would dress in brown woollen tunics and trousers and slip into their soft leather boots. Ro-Gan was a good student and enjoyed more freedom in the underground settlement than most, of course he was not trusted as much as any of the half-breeds and certainly not as much as any of his orc masters. However, he had come learn that the Orsk were a dying breed since magic, the thing that seemed to have bound them all together was dissipating from the earth.

Unbeknown to Ro-Gan was a place called 'the breeding pits' chambers where human females lived and who were habitually raped by the Orsk and whose babies would become the foundation for the future of the Orsk race and who were called by their Orsk masters, the half-breeds.

Ro-Gan was one of only a few boys who could both speak and write Ingolandic, the common human language of the Shattered Kingdoms and as he taught is best friend On-Gar the half-breed how to read and write, he in turn taught Ro-Gan, Wiaznuri, or black speech, the language of the orcs. Ro-

Gan also spoke the language of the elves, but he was yet to actually meet one to converse with so that part of his education he kept to himself.

Most nights, Ro-Gan would struggle to get straight off to sleep and his hours were broken with wild dreams of Elves and men, sometimes he would see the face of a woman who he called mother but that face never had features it was always blurred, then on other occasions he would be practicing sword craft with a man who dressed in the finest armour.

One of the reasons that the boys were told to paint themselves with the green dye was to deter them from trying to escape when they were allowed outside to hunt for food or they were involved in a raid, but as raids were predominantly carried out at night under the cover of darkness, Ro-Gan figured you couldn't actually tell what colour any body's skin was, they were all just a filthy brownish as it was hard to keep that clean, but he followed orders, not because he wanted to, far from it, from the first evening he was captured and dragged here, down to this very day, Ro-Gan plotted his escape, and as he got to know all the other captive boys he figured he take them all with him too.

The boys were from all backgrounds and all within a couple of years of each other in age, Ro-Gan was fifteen as he had counted down the years of his captivity. The half-breeds were mostly older by a couple of years but that was not true in every case. Each human captive was paired with a half-breed and together they learned to fight, they ate, worked together and they slept in the same cave dwelling. It was not an idea mix but Ro-Gan was a charismatic boy who was determined to pull everyone together while he plotted and planned their great escape. Sometimes he would talk about escape with the half-breeds as well and to his surprise, none of them ever told the orcs of his plans.

Today though was not a normal day, a normal day would consist of the whole band of boys and half-breeds working hard at the settlements forges all morning making swords, daggers, helmets and plate armour and the like, which was taken away and never seen again, even the Orsk local to the settlement never used any of the equipment they made not even while in the outside world, it was the first of many a puzzle that Ro-Gan had no idea the answer. All of the settlements equipment in fact came from what they stole or won on raids. However, today was the day of the coming-of-age ceremony and there was great excitement throughout the settlement, even amongst the Orsk.

Ro-Gan's thoughts were interrupted by the sudden appearance of the Orsk chief, Snag-Roth.

Snag-Roth was a likable type even for an Orsk, most of the other orcs were cruel by nature and most definitely aloof in character, Snag-Roth was easy going and only seemed to want a quiet life arranging the affairs of his charges. He stood a little over five feet in Hight which seemed to be an average height for the orcs that Ro-Gan had seen. His age was unknown but if the scars on his face and upper arms were anything to go by. He had certainly lived a full and exerting life, perhaps this was where old orc warriors ended their days babysitting young captives.

"Ro-Gan, On-Gar, get dressed for the day and follow me, quickly!" barked Snag-Roth.

"Where do we go in such a hurry?" Ro-Gan inquired, knowing full well where they would be taken. On-Gar was very excited and looking forward to testing his metal. Ro-Gan was just as excited but was trying his hardest to be indifferent in front of others.

Snag-Roth spoke quietly to Ro-Gan, "You have been training now with us for five winters. It is time to for you to prove you are a warrior. It is your coming-of-age ceremony. You too, On-Gar!" he called as they hambled down the tunnel that connected their space with the main arena, a great cavernous space at the centre of the settlement.

Now all the human boys and their half-breed companions are gathered. And it would seem not just from Ro-Gan's part of the settlement but from the other two areas as well. Thirty-six boys along with thirty six half-breeds, each pair being matched up to fight another pair, each are then given weapons, exact replicas of the real thing, but made from bone, it might have been wood but for the fact that not a single tree grew within leagues of this place, if hit by anyone of these implements, they could brake bone or at the very least bruise the flesh heavily.

Above the arena was a wooden walkway that ran all around the circumference of the cave and it slowly started to fill up with other Orsk. They were all very eager to see how their young charges would fair in combat. The mood was very upbeat and in Ro-Gan's five winters here he had never seen anything like it, many Orsk shouted for certain young ones who they had come to know personally, and many bets began to change hands and much drink was being consumed.

Chief Snag-Roth shouted for silence as the noise was beginning to reach fever pitch.

"The rules of the competition are simple, put your opponent down by any means, if your companion goes down

31

and is unable to continue, he will fight alone in the next round."

"After the first round is over, you will be given five minutes to gather yourselves for the next round, the round of forty-eight."

"The third round will be contested by those twenty-four who come through the forty-eight and will be given a ten-minute rest period."

"The fourth round will be contested by those winning twelve, and they will be given a full fifteen-minute rest period."

"The six couples who make it to the fifth round will enjoy a half-hour brake, when the fighting commences you will notice a new team will have been added, give a cheer now and again when Chiefs Lug-Ran and Bal-Dok grace the arena with their mighty show of strength and agility." The upper balcony erupted with shouts and cheers while those who were about to fight stayed silent.

"The last two standing who reach the final will then fight each other; the winner will be declared the leader of this new warband."

"Let the fight begin!" shouted another Orsk chief from somewhere up on the wooden walkway.

The contestants had been paired-up they lined up outside the arena and the first four names were called.

By the time it was Ro-Gan's turn, eight fighters had been eliminated one with a broken arm another with blood pouring from a face wound. Ro-Gan took moved to the other side of the arena and took his stand broadsword in hand, On-Gar was at his left side, he had chosen a war-axe. Their opponents looked tense, continually shifting their weight from one foot to the other. The chief Orsk clanged a small hammer on the side of the arena signalling that the fight should begin.

Straight away one of the other two lurched forward towards Ro-Gan with his weapon of choice, a long mace, held high over his head. Ro-Gan weighted a moment before crouching down, his weight on the ball of his right foot and his left leg outstretched, as the fighter drew level with his left foot, Ro-Gan swirled his body around broadsword in hand in low slicing cut from his right to left.

The other fighter was trying to bring his weapon down on top of Ro-Gan head when the broadsword hit his left cracking the bone clean in two, if it had been a proper sword the opponent would have lost both legs such was the force behind the swing.

On-Gar's opponent was suddenly caught in two minds, which was a fast take down of his teammate, he too was using a clubbed weapon, and attempting to drive it downward from over his own head. On-Gar took advantage of the indecision and ran sideways at him with his war-axe firmly clenched in both hands as he swiped with force into the gut of his opponent.

Both competitors were down writhing in agony, the match was over.

Being early in the draw, it gave Ro-Gan and On-Gar the ability to watch the others and make mental note of how they fought. It was about another hour before round two began and this time they had been drawn against an opponent who partner had been knocked out in the last round, so he faced them alone. This time, On-Gar made the first move by stepping forward bowing to the single opponent before placing his war-axe on the floor just Infront of his feet. The opponent smiled before launching his attack, his blade thrust forward in a full-frontal attack, quick as a flash On-Gar curled his right foot around the shaft of the axe, flicked it into the air, twirled it three times and then threw it at the oncoming opponent hitting square on the forehead. The unfortunate attacker hit the ground face first and was knocked out completely. Two rounds left.

After the second round, all those couples who were left were allowed a quick water brake and a few minutes to recover. There was not one of those surviving competitors who wasn't covered in bruises or welts from head to toe.

In this next fight, the orc chief allowed the contestants to take their starting positions before he threw only two weapons into the arena, a broadsword and a short sword. As soon as the competitors heard the clang, Ro-Gan's opponent threw himself to the centre ground right arm outstretched clutching for the longer sword.

Ro-Gan did a move similar to one of his earlier bouts. He crouched low but instead of placing his left leg out for balance, this time he swept it around catching his opponent just has he had clasped his right hand around the broadsword.

The force of Ro-Gan's kick knocked the blade straight to the feet of On-Gar who picked it up and began twirling it around in his right hand while in sighting his opposite number to dare attack without a weapon. Ro-Gan was still swirling around low to the ground when he caught On-Gar's opponent with a hard kick to the back of his calf.

As the stunned opponent turned to look at Ro-Gan, On-Gar ran forward and cracked him on the side of the head with the blunted broadsword, once more knocking his opponent clean out.

The round of the last six began the two half-breed chiefs were added to the contest, fortunately they were not Ro-Gan and On-Gar's opponents.

Ro-Gan and On-Gar exchanged a few brief words before the clang of the chief's hammer rang out. Ro-Gan immediate grabbed On-Gars left arm which was raised up towards On-Gar face as he clenched both hands tightly around On-Gar fist he was lifted off his feet and his legs were carrying him in a circular motion around On-Gar and back towards his opponent.

As he moved forward unsure quite what was happening as this bout was without weapons, On-Gar heaved Ro-Gan forward, Ro-Gan clasped his legs around the half-breed's neck before dropping the rest of his body like a dead weight towards the floor.

The half-breed was propelled forward headfirst over Ro-Gan and into the floor where On-Gar gave him an almighty great kick in the solar plexus, one down one to go. This time, it was On-Gar who took the lead by running around back of the human opponent as Ro-Gan feigned a frontal attack.

The human ignored On-Gar fearing Ro-Gan as the better fighter, and so he girded his loins and stood with his fists raised. However, to his surprise Ro-Gan threw himself down at his feet just before On-Gar drop kicked him from behind. Ro-Gan quickly cupped his arm around the human's head and tried to suffocate him.

The human was very strong and grabbed hold of Ro-Gan's arm and slowly started to pull it away so that he could catch his breath. It was at this point that On-Gar improvised and seeing the very real danger that this opponent would soon be on his feet he kicked him with all his might right between the legs.

The Orsk whose number had been growing around the arena suddenly began whooping and cheering this had been the best entertainment they had seen in a long time.

The next round came and went just as the last one had and has fate would seem to be the master of ceremonies, Ro-Gan and On-Gar met Lug-Ran and Bal-Dok in the final. Both newcomers were already battle harden warriors and to make things worse they had only fought in a couple of the previous bouts, so they were relatively fresh.

Ro-Gan spoke quickly with On-Gar telling him that these two fought more like orcs than humans or indeed the other half-breeds, so they would be all about front attack and brawn over brains, Ro-Gan and On-Gar needed to be smarter and faster, Ro-Gan intermated a fighting style that they had been training and practicing for weeks. It was supposed to be used in their escape attempt but it would equally work here Ro-Gan thought.

The contest went on for much longer than any of the orcs had envisaged including the two who were fighting and there constant insistence of running straight at Ro-Gan and On-Gar was beginning to tell on them as their strength ebbed away, Shields drooped on arms and weapons were not held as high for the sweeping cuts, again On-Gar grabbed hold of Ro-Gan's left forearm and was lifted in the air high enough to kick Bal-Dok full in the face as he failed to raise his shield in time.

One down, one to go, Lu-Ran had learned nothing it seemed and his attack was straight forward yet again, and the outcome was just the same. Ro-Gan side stepped and parried

Lug-Ran's war-axe, and On-Gar got around the back of him and hit him in the lower back with a mighty blow to his lower back. Lug-Ran was beaten, and he felt to his knees screaming a blood curdling noise that acknowledged his defeat.

The final saw Ro-Gan pitted against On-Gar for the right to be called War-Chief, but On-Gar had no desire either to fight his friend nor did he want the responsibility of being a War-Chief.

Nevertheless, the rules were the rules and the two had to fight each other without weapons. Ro-Gan soon started to feel On-Gar's strength sapping as they wrestled each other this way and that, and the next time they both fell to the ground arms and legs entangled Ro-Gan was able to gain purchase with his legs around On-Gar's neck while holding his left arm out and up causing On-Gar to immediately slap his right hand down on the floor in submission.

Fifteen-year-old Ro-Gan was cheered by all that were present including when he looked up some of the Orsk masters, but the result also began a feeling of hatred amongst both the defeated and the other Orsk masters. The rules were the rules and Ro-Gan had won fairly and squarely, and so the newly appointed War-Chief was presented with a set of chain armour, a leather under jerkin, arm grieves and leg grieves and belt, along with a sharp edged broadsword and round shield, On-Gar was suitably attired and was called first gedriht, this meant Ro-Gan's number two in command of the newly formed warband.

Gedriht was the name of those who form the chief's personal bodyguard and in this warband it would consist of twelve from those boys and half-breeds who won their first-round bouts, all of the others would henceforth be called Geoguth.

All of the Gedriht were equipped with helmet and chainmail along with a shield, broadsword and two-and-a-half-metre long spear. The Geoguth had the best of the rest equipment wise, older segmented or leather armour and a bucket helmet or leather cap and there would be armed with a short stabbing sword, a shield and spear.

Later as the ranks swelled some of the warriors might gain a higher status, that of Duguth, or veteran warrior and other additional warrior types like skirmishers who would only wear leather armour and caps, and have daggers, slings or composite bows.

The rest of this evening, Ro-Gan would take to get to know his followers made up equally of humans and half-breeds there was food and drink aplenty and even the older orc chiefs would be seen to walk amongst them, although the new warband were not treated as equals they had certainly earned the respect of their Orsk masters.

During one such interaction, Ro-Gan asked one of the Orsk chiefs why they had to dye their skin each morning, to which he was told so that if they did escape the tunnels and run back to the humans then they would be treated as hostiles and probably killed, it was as he had suspected. Ro-Gan quickly moved the conversation along not wanting to dwell on the thoughts of escape and that unhappy conclusion. Ro-Gan wanted to gain the secrets, he wanted answers, nothing much up until now made any sense, this whole underground set up, Orsk were never this intelligent nor were they ever this organised even when magic was strong in the world his hunger for escape would have to be checked for the time being at least. There was a far deeper mystery a foot and it had ensnared the boy completely.

The following day, Ro-Gan was putting his warriors through their paces and speaking to them each in turn about what they could expect and what he ultimately expected from them. Later that day while all the warriors were taken to their work duties, Ro-Gan was taken to meet a new Orsk he had not seen before. This Orsk was old and gnarled with many scars to show for his years. WarLord, Poda-Gog.

Huge like a bear and five foot six or seven, but he was fascinating for another reason other than his scars, for he was decorated with much gold unlike any of the other orcs Ro-Gan had met so far. Gold arm bracelets that went the length of his forearm, and chains that huge thickly around his neck. At his side was a huge war-hammer discoloured by a large amount of dried blood and dirt from many a battle Ro-Gan imagined.

Poda-Gog, wanted to talk about a fourth coming raid and was explaining the night mission Ro-Gan was to take his warband on, it involved attacking a troop of border guards (Human), that were traversing a main road between two towns that Ro-Gan had never heard of before. His brief was to take out the fighters whether they were male or female, capture any children and to take any weapons or armour and of course bring back any other loot. It was imperative that the mission was to take place at night, so timing was everything, and so that the humans would believe it was an Orsk warband, which Ro-Gan didn't quite understand at the time but excepted, and it was also imperative that if they took any casualties that they were to be brought back also, on no account must the humans suspect what has happened.

Ro-Gan's curiosity was growing ever more suspicious when he was handed a folded goat skin square which turned out to be a map. Now Ro-Gan had been schooled by monks in a lot of things but never had he heard that Orsk plan anything in this detail or use maps for what was supposed to be an ordinary raid, they had a language, but it was not one that be written down as such.

Even more mystery enveloped the inner workings of Ro-Gan's mind, to have sleepless nights over, but for now he was going to have to put his thoughts and emotions to one side and just follow orders. However, it made him even more determined to liberate all the captives and put pay to whatever evil was going on.

Ro-Gan lead his warband of twenty four, half-human and of half-breeds, out from the depth and safety of the tunnels for the very first time as their leader, and as he emerged from the torch lit interior to the moon lit exterior, he saw that they were at the base of a great mountain range and before them lay a great and vast expanse of undulating, partially frozen tundra.

The night air was bitter, and each warrior shivered as they acclimatised to it themselves, Ro-Gan who was wearing his new (well reclaimed new) armour, took the goatskin map from his trouser pocket and studied it for a moment. Some of the warriors who had earned nothing in combat wore only their tunic and trousers and who had rusty old swords and battered small wooden shields. They were truly shivering to the bone and therefore more eager than most to get moving.

The road that they needed to be on was far to the south west and it looked as though it lay across what could have been a border line, perhaps a neighbouring realm more than that Ro-Gan did not know, in point of fact, he had no idea where he was at all, even if he was still in some part of the Shattered Realms or not. All he did know was that the target were humans, and they were trained in combat to some degree, but he was assured by Poda-Gog that were no match for Ro-Gan's highly trained warriors.

Orsk warbands were expected to run far and to move swiftly so without further ado they were on the move keeping the high mountains to there right as they travelled straight down following a well-used but poorly maintained track. The journey took what was left of the twilight and not once did they spot another soul nor did they see a single dwelling place, nor even a tree, but all along the length of the mountains, they saw what could easily have been more concealed tunnel entrances just like the one they had come from. This made Ro-Gan wonder just how many more encampments like his were there.

The border between the two realms was marked by a rather crude set of wooden posts that had dried out and cracked in many places, dead wood just like this whole landscape apart from the wild grass, and a ditch that contained nothing more than a trickle of water under a frozen canopy.

None of the posts, on closer examination looked cut rather they resembled naturally fallen branches or driftwood from the beach that he knew was nearby somewhere in the opposite direction to what they travelled now.

The fence in places looked like there once might have been barbed wire between the posts but not so much remained today but what did was pock marked with clumps of wool so there must have been sheep in this area at one time, or maybe there still was but he couldn't hear or see any at this time.

It was easy to jump the ditch for all but one, one of the half-bloods, called Sugg, he was one of the Geoguth, the ones who were eliminated in the first round of the competition, sadly he was not in the greatest of health and he was wide at the girth and of very limited intelligence, and if anyone was going to, it was he who slipped as he tried to jump and he landed heavily on the far bank were the others were assembled, his left leg sliding into the freezing water. Sugg yelped like a scolded puppy at the shock of the cold water which made all of the others have to stifle laughter, Ro-Gan hissed for quite as he walked forward towards the stricken warrior and bent down to offer his hand.

"We are no longer in an area where we can count on support even at night, so from here on in, we must muffle our weapons and hold our tongues, the target area is still quite a way head, roughly two leagues away and the sun will be rising before we arrive if we drag our feet."

The road marked on the map turned out to be well maintained and although there were no buildings in sight in any direction Ro-Gan observed that this was a main road, perhaps it joined military outposts as it followed the lay of the land that ran parallel to what he thought was the boarder.

They came a little way along the road, Ro-Gan was obviously looking for something, but he was well aware of the time as the sky began to lighten in the far east.

The spot Ro-Gan had eventually chosen gave cover to his warband in a ditch that ran either side of the road, but this side had a small coppice of trees in which the warriors could hide. As the sun began to climb in the eastern sky, the vibration of feet on road were felt by one of the half-breeds who lay with his head to the ground, and he signalled to Ro-Gan before On-Gar ushered everyone to their positions.

From the east, the hazy figures emerged walking slowly along the road it could be seen that there were at least three ox-drawn wagons with them and after a few moments it could be counted that there were soldiers, none of whom wore any kind of armour, but each did hold a spear and a small round shield known as a 'buckler'. It was a mistake to ambush the soldiers here because they had the sun at their backs even though it was still very low in the eastern sky, but Ro-Gan would never make this mistake again.

The soldiers were all wearing woollen tunics in various shades of yellow with slightly darker brown trousers, possibly where the dye has run from being out in the pour rain, the lot of a soldier is not a glamorous one Ro-Gan mused to himself, each had feet shod in leather sandals but again it was noted by Ro-Gan that they made a sort of clipping sound on the surface of the road, the sandals he later would discover had flat metal nails driven in to them.

Ro-Gan saw a very solemn and sorry looking bunch of older men and boys who were even younger than he was, and as they came more into view, he determined that their number was twelve, so including the waggoneers their total number eighteen.

As the column drew level with Ro-Gan's hiding place, he could clearly see six men out front, three wagons and six men at the rear, and all completely oblivious to what was about to unfold.

On-Gar stood up from his concealed spot and roared at the top if his voice before hurling his spear into the flank of the lead oxen, of the six men out front three dropped their weapons and shields and threw themselves to the ground in sheer terror. The other three stood transfixed at this mighty warrior baring his (dyed green) chest and launching his spear, which looked a lot longer and thicker than the ones they carried.

There was no time to think, now was the moment the rest of the warband rose and attacked the soldiers, each picking a single target and launching their spears at that target. The lead ox which was struck heavily by the spear bayed in pain and tore forward almost dragging the other ox with it and the front six soldiers were trampled and became entangled with the oxen and by the trailing leather straps. They died a terrible slow death many with mangled and broken bodies and who were defenceless against the long spears now being poke and prodded at them.

The front wagon lurched up as one of the heavy iron-shod wooden wheels ran over one of the soldiers and it tipped on its side eventually as it cleared the stricken bodies and was gently helped over by a couple of the warband. The second wagon was turned by its driver but went straight down into the ditch on the opposite side of the road, causing the wagon to go over on its side and spilling the two soldiers out. One tumbled head first into the ditch wall breaking his neck instantly and the other was pitched forward between the two oxen, he died an agonising death as the two frightened beasts tried in vain to extricate themselves from the ditch and repeatedly trampling over the human.

The remaining six soldiers ran up alongside the third wagon neither knowing whether to defend it or themselves and they each died from spear and sword wounds. The whole melee lasted no more than a few short seconds but at the time to Ro-Gan it felt a lot longer, four wounded prisoners were brought before him as the rest of the warband set about looting the wagons.

Ro-Gan wanted to know who these men were and where they were from and what was the reason for them being on this road at this time, the first captured man, one of the older looking soldiers refused to utter a single word, he just stared defiantly, and he was put to the sword by one of the half-breed warriors, Ro-Mir, who, when he realised that Ro-Gan was staring straight at him in utter debrief, could only manage to say, 'my bad', before walking away and hiding amongst the others.

The second human saw this barbaric act and began to whimper like a beaten puppy, and when Ro-Gan stepped towards him and began to question him, the human was hard to silence in the end. Ro-Gan spoke in the language of the human, who was surprised at first and although the prisoner's speech was heavily accented, Rogan began to picture where he was.

This country was called, Lōrnicā, which from the location on his map, the prisoner was able to say that Ro-Gan was from the neighbouring country of Obreā, when he said the name he spat at Ro-Gan's feet. On-Gar slapped the back of his head and told him to show some respect, and although On-Gar spoke the human language, but this dialect was hard for him to follow or to speak himself properly, and so the man understood nothing of why he had been hit.

The last two prisoners were two young boys around Ro-Gan's own age, one was called, Brenn and the other, Willem. They had been the two atop the third wagon and although they were so young, they had jumped down into the melee in aid

45

of their comrades and Ro-Gan was impressed by their spirit, his men didn't seem to be too aggressive towards them either had they had not inflicted anything more than wounded pride on any of the warband, and part of the orders stipulated the capture of young prisoners.

The older man was released after questioning as Ro-Gan's orders were to do just so, his master had said that someone needed to tell the other humans that they had been attacked and by orcs. 'Fear is the key' was all Poda-Gog would say, over and over again.

The two boys were to be brought back, again, as instructed as Ro-Gan and so many other boys were as future warriors. Both the boys were scared witless at what had happened and probably at this point thought that they would soon be roasted over an open fire and eaten, Ro-Gan saw the fear in their eyes but for now there was nothing he could do to allay those fears and so he did nothing apart from bound and gag them.

The six oxen were released from their harnesses and chased away while the three wagons with had by now been completely looted were pushed into the ditch as close together as they could. All of the dead humans had been piled on top of the middle wagon and then the wagons were set on fire. Everything the warband could possibly carry was stuffed into haversacks.

The journey back to the tunnels in Obreā was a little slower partly because by now the sun was high up in the midday sky and it was punishingly hot with no building or trees or other shady places, added to that all of the contraband that was taken was beginning to weigh them all down and rations were running low since Ro-Gan insisted that the two boys be kept well fed and watered regularly.

Every step forward was a step nearer to home and Ro-Gan's mood lightened somewhat, and he had removed the gags from the two boy's mouths and began to chat to them partly to allay their fears and because the idea would be that they will soon be joining his warband as his follows.

Once Brenn and Willem had got over the shock of this overtly friendly orc, and the fact that they still had not been eaten, they both began to ask questions of Ro-Gan and why they were spared when some many of the others were not. Ro-Gan grumbled that he only been following orders but that this will all begin to make more sense in the future especially if they did as they told and kept close to his side. Two more humans even added to his warband would make it uneven and already there were murmurings of unrest at the humans.

On-Gar joined in with the conversation from time-to-time, as he started to pick up some of the more familiar words that Ro-Gan had taught him. For the last five years he had craved everything that Ro-Gan had to teach him, and now he felt confident enough to engage another human in conversation. On-Gar did not have any prejudices and truth beknown didn't see himself as any different to Ro-Gan, they were both born to a woman and but for the colour of their respective skins they were equals or sorts.

On-Gar wanted to saviour every waking moment of this mission, outside with his comrades, free from any watching Orsk masters and second only to Ro-Gan in the chain of command. This was certainly a life style he could start getting used to. He hated being in the tunnels and he hated the fact that he didn't make it into the ranks of the black guard, nothing to do with his fighting prowess, but because he was three inches to short, every Black Guard candidate had to be at least six foot in height, nothing else mattered, they could be as stupid as the day was long so long as they fit the height requirement.

Shortly after the warband had crossed the broken border markers and while Ro-Gan was still deep in conversation with the two boys, Brenn the younger of the two, spoke candidly.

"I know you are not orcs."

On-Gar was the first to react. "Of course we are orcs!" he said before raising his hands above the young one and baring his teeth and making his fingers like claws.

Which Brenn did not see but Willem did, and it made him laugh.

"We are green are we not?" retorted Ro-Gan.

"Yes, you are green but your eyes are like my own and your teeth aren't sharp and pointy, and you still haven't eaten us!"

"We haven't eaten you yet!" replied an astonished On-Gar.

"My grandfather taught me all about Orsk and he described them to me in perfect detail."

"Ah, so you are like an expert Orsk 'knower', are you, little one?" asked Ro-Gan, highly amused with the game that they were playing.

Willem turned around to walk backwards so that he could face his cousin Brenn, Ro-Gan and On-Gar. "Who are you actually because my cousin is right, look at your clothes especially where they have got damp from sweat."

Ro-Gan and On-Gar both looked down at the tunics where the chainmail didn't cover the material, and where the sweat had mixed with the dye from their skin, the cloth was stained green. "Neither do you growl like Orsk when they speak, and

I don't mean when your friend there was being silly wiggling his fingers around and sticking out his tongue."

Ro-Gan spoke directly to the two boys now and he lowered his voice so that nobody other than On-Gar could hear, "The truth is that I was captured years ago just like you both and On-Gar here helped me to survive while I taught him to read and write and all about the outside world. We work for the orcs but to what end we have no idea but we have fought our way to the top and have been given this warband so we intend to follow our orders until we can find out what is really happening, will you two join our warband and help us two to find the answers we seek?"

Both boys looked at each other and without a word spoken nodded in agreement. Brenn, the younger of the cousins, said that his father might be able to help, in fact he went on, "If you let us both go then I could ask my father to bring his army to help break you free."

Ro-Gan smiled at the innocence of youth, not that he was any older by much. "So, who might your father be that he can call on an army?"

Willem, the older boy, told Brenn to 'shut up' before he turned to Ro-Gan and spoke some more, "His father, my uncle is the chieftain of a village about a league from where you attacked us and those men you killed were some of his soldiers."

"They aren't very good then are they, they didn't even manage to wound one of us!" On-Gar chipped in, looking very smug as he did so.

"He is a very rich man and he could pay mercenaries to hunt you down and rescue us!" said Brenn.

"Yeah, in fact it was only recently that a man came from Råvenniå to offer my uncle mercenaries to fight for him," Willem stated.

Ro-Gan flashed a look of puzzlement at On-Gar and kept his own council when he wondered if this far north you would need to even have an army. Lōrnicā, Ro-Gan knew from his studies was in the far north of the Shattered Kingdoms and the countries below it were all allies, or at least from what he could recall they were.

"Tell me, boys, how often did your army encounter anyone who wanted to fight it?" Ro-Gan asked.

"Never!" shouted Brenn. "Well, not in our lifetime, anyway, but now you have perhaps my uncle will buy those mercenaries after all." Suddenly, it was Willems turn to be smug.

Ro-Gan became more curiouser by the moment, was this part of a bigger picture, who were these mercenaries? Were Ro-Gan and his warband making arms and armour for them? Did the Orsk know about them, was that why they were birthing the half-bloods, to even up the odds? Every question brought up more and more questions and no immediate answers and Ro-Gan was becoming increasingly frustrated.

Just before the sun had fallen in the west, the warband had reached the gapping tunnel mouth that marked their return to the large cave at the centre of the tunnels they now called home, as the warband filed in down the first corridor and out into the arena many of the Orsk who roamed the upper walkways, gathered and began to cheer and bang the blunt side of their weapons on the walkway railings.

The biggest cheer was saved for when each of the warband soldiers emptied their canvas sacks of all the loot they had recovered and then when the two boys were pushed down onto their knees just behind all of the loot.

"You have done very well, Ro-Gan, and as well you who are members of his warband!" bellowed the Orsk, Snag-Roth.

After a moment or two of complete silence, Chief Snag-Roth signalled to his left, it was a sort of circling of his hand ending with his index finger pointing down at the spoils of the raid. Out of one of the tunnels, a group of four Orsk waddled to picked through the loot for weapons and shields, they split the things gathered, into two piles, one half of which they then picked up as best they could and then took it and disappeared down the tunnel, they had come from leaving the other pile just as it were.

"Ro-Gan, take these weapons and share them with your warriors, but do not give anything to those two boys, you must now decide who amongst your warriors will be rewarded with the best equipment and if any who should be left out, that is the way of the orc."

Ro-Gan picked up each weapon and shield in turn and weighted it in his mind and swished a few different swords through the air to test their weight and balance before singling one or other warrior out from his warband and handing the item to them.

The Orsk chief waited until Ro-Gan had finished before summoning yet another four orcs from another tunnel. "Take all of the woollen garment, pelts, furs and other material things and separate them into two piles," Snag-Roth barked.

This was a slow deliberate demonstration of how things would work hence forth until there was nothing left to divide up, Then Ro-Gan asked what he should do with the two captives.

The chief said that they should be taken to the place where all of the settlement's captive women were housed until they could be placed in a settlement as new warriors, either that or their relatives could pay a handsome reward for their safe return, the last bit of his sentence made the old orc laugh and his laughter was joined by many others, as human coins meant nothing to orcs unless they could be used to melt down and be made into bracelets of rank.

After everything that needed to be done was done, Snag-Roth called for any other business.

"Forgive me, Lord Chief, but there is but one thing I have withheld from you, and you have just reminded me, for I do not know if it has any value here," Ro-Gan spoke loudly up to the gallery.

"Whatever are you rambling on about?" asked the chief Orsk.

"Lord Chief, I collected many small coins, here in this purse, but I do not know if you value them as the humans do?" Ro-Gan said placatingly.

The Orsk chief once more summoned from the tunnel a single Orsk who walked purposefully over to Ro-Gan and took the purse from him. He then tipped the coins on to the floor at Ro-Gan's feet and stood looking at them all, he counted thirty individual pieces; five of which were gold, nine were silver and the rest bronze and copper. The Orsk grunted and then picked up the gold and silver coins but left the others where they had fallen before walking off back down the tunnel he had come from.

"Ro-Gan, sort the bronze coins from the copper ones, and then smelt the bronze down to make individual bracelets for you and your most trusted warriors, one each mind, that will show your rank amongst the others of your kind. The copper which is the least value must be made into bracelets for the other warriors who fought well but did nothing outstanding, and for those who gained nothing this time, well, to you I say, fight harder next time! Now go, I have to report your return to those who sit above me in rank."

Three days had passed before Ro-Gan and On-Gar were summoned to the Orsk chief once more. His cave was first up a set of carved stairs and then turn right towards the balcony above the arena. The cave had been carved into the wall just off the upstairs balcony and it had a rather crude wooden wall and an ill fitted door. The wood was not unlike that which was used for the border posted, bleach, dried out, and pitted with gaps in between so that it offered some privacy but not that much so that you couldn't hear every word that was being spoken inside.

The orc guard who had brought Ro-Gan and On-Gar to the door, stopped, and then knocked four times, and was beckoned inside.

"Ah, good here you are, have the two boys been returned to your care, of course they have, their kinfolk decided the ransom we offered was agreeable, but we reneged on the deal but still took the coin."

"Can I ask why, chief?"

"You just did but I do not have to give you an answer, I should have you flogged for insubordination, that's what I should do!"

Ro-Gan said nothing and just stared straight ahead.

"Oh, don't sulk now, there is nothing worse than a sulking human, in all of my experience they tend to be even more useless than when they are happy, I will say it is all part of a bigger picture, which you and On-Gar are now part of."

This time, Ro-Gan half smiled and nodded his head.

"Now, tell me both do you; how does it feel to wear your bracelets of rank?" the Orsk chief enquired.

"Bracelet of rank?" Ro-Gan looked bemused.

The chief cackled as a wry smile broke out across his deeply lined face. "But of course, you have no idea, each warrior wears a bracelet of rank, Gold being the highest, silver the second, bronze the third and copper the lowest, so you see you two are now able to move more freely and have more privileges around our little kingdom under the mountains."

3 Escape

Ro-Gan was being trusted more and more and allowed to go further and further away from the sanctuary of the tunnels, all be it to find food and fetch it back but he knew he was winning the orcs trust, and it was rewarded one day when Snag-Roth called him to follow him up a second flight of stairs and to another cave off a main corridor, this one though had a fine wooden front and a better fitting door. Snag-Roth knocked but did not wait to be invited in, instead he opened the door for Ro-Gan who saw that it was the Lord Chief's room.

Lord Chief began his conversation by teasing Ro-Gan, saying that if he had the chance he would run away, even after all the Orsk had done for him.

"Where would we go, Lord Chief. What else is there to see beyond what we have seen already?" asked Ro-Gan.

When the Orsk boss replied, this time Ro-Gan detected some reticence in his voice.

"We are but a small settlement, the settlement of Nedrakah, Nedrakah is in fact my name, before your success you had not earned the right even to know that, and now you do!"

"Are there more settlements like this, Lord Chief Nedrakah?"

"I am the master of two more settlements just like this one but I am not allowed to have any more than 100 warriors at my command at any given time, and I also lay claim to one birthing chamber with thirty human birth mothers, who when in child service the needs of the settlement with strong young half-breeds."

Ro-Gan was horrified to hear the last part of the chief's statement, but he gave nothing away and he remained on the outside impassive. "Why do we never see the human women, Lord Chief?"

"They are a commodity, we breed with them, they raise the half-breeds until we harvest them, they are not there for our self-gratification, although it is something I know that humans value, never the less, you would see them and take pity on them, I have seen how you fuss over some of your warriors, you are like a mother hen cluck, clucking, Ro-Gan?"

"Yes, of course!" replied Ro-Gan barely able to maintain his composure.

"Anyway, go now take On-Gar with you, go and explore just don't wander too far you have another mission tomorrow."

Ro-Gan and On-Gar ventured down one of the tunnels that the Orsk had come from earlier, at the other end were two large Orsk guards, they held a small shield each but a long-shafted spear which bore, just below the bladed edge, two small axe heads, one either side. On seeing the two newcomers, the guards quickly crossed their weapons in order to stop the advancing pair.

"Halt! Are you two lost or do you both just have a death wish?" said one guard in the language of the Orsk, not expecting either to understand him, his fellow guard just laughed.

Ro-Gan held out his left arm to show his newly acquired bronze bracelet.

Both guards laughed once more and more heartily this time before stamping their feet and clanging their spear tips together.

A voice no less gruff came from behind the two guards and just enough in the darkness so that neither Ro-Gan nor On-Gar could see who spoke, but it was enough to make the two guards leap aside and stand to attention.

"You must be the new pair, the ones who all the fuss is about, and now I can see why!" said the voice as the form of another half-orc came into view.

"Snag-Roth's pet, my oh my, such wealth you flaunt it is no wonder these poor guards are in shock."

"We were told that it would be ok for us to explore," Ro-Gan explained.

"So, it is Hu-man, so it is, and you are welcome to meet with my warband," the figure said, completely ignoring On-Gar who in his eyes brought shame on his race by only coming second. The shapeless figure stepped forward into the light of the lit torch above Ro-Gan.

"I am Bal-Dok, we met in the arena, remember, and as you can see, I have a silver bracelet which makes me your senior!"

Ro-Gan and On-Gar moved freely amongst Bal-Dok's warband meeting and greeting each man and half-breed in turn, looking at their impressive bracelets and jewel encrusted necklaces, most of the half-breeds just ignored them or spoke curtly in Black speech, some glanced over and then away as if uninterested in the slightest. One or two, however, did ask how many battles had Ro-Gan or On-Gar fought in, and still others asked how many winters they had been here for, a reply was expected as nobody thought for one minute they could be understood, it was as though On-Gar was a human as well, or had been corrupted and made deaf or mute or both.

The uneasy peace of this part of the cave network was shattered when a blood curdling cry went up from one corner of the settlements large cave followed by a name that was repeatedly being called out in orcish. "Aatu! Aatu! Aatu!"

The humans and half-breeds parted as the short wild looking creature moved through the rank and file, pushing a shoving as it made its way towards Ro-Gan. Bal-Dok had spotted the commotion and swiftly made his way to a spot just between the creature and Ro-Gan.

"Berba-Shin, what is all this noise and especially on the eve of battle, are you not supposed to be on our side?" cried the half-breed chief in mock outrage.

"Aatu, where is Aatu?" the creature begged.

Berba-Shin shuffled into view and for the first time Ro-Gan stood face-to-face with an orc shaman and the last surviving orc female, as far as any Orsk could be sure. She was dishevelled and her skin although still green was pitted with dirt and dry blood and she smelled like she had slept all her life in a crypt. Atop her head sat a skull headdress slightly to one side as it had slipped forward and entangled in her greasy mop of long straggly white hair, as she choose to speak her words in Ro-Gan's language non but On-Gar and the other humans from Bal-Dok's warband could understand her, even so, none could work out why she repeatedly asked after 'Aatu', which literary just mean noble wolf.

Bal-Dok meant what he had said about the commotion being caused on the eve of battle and especially since he had no idea what the old hag was saying. Bad enough he had to be courteous to this stinking human, but this was beyond the pale. "Go! Now, Berba-Shin we must spend our evening together as brothers for some this will be their last evening, instead of this racket why not bless my fine warriors with the blood of the sacrifices you have made?"

"Stupid half-breed! If I took the time to relieve myself on you all, it would be a blessing." With that, Berba-Shin scurried away muttering to herself in Ingolandic one minute and then black speech the next and cackling in between, as she disappeared into the deep dark recesses of the tunnels, and after a few moments of complete silence Bal-Dok raised a goblet of ale and shouted praise be to Ares, the God of war, and a great cheer went up that reverberated around the cavernous space, which rose even louder as everyone present joined in with the name chanting.

On-Gar turned to Ro-Gan and asked in hushed tones if it were better, they go now before the whole ceiling collapses.

"Why did she approach you in such a way Ro-Gan, she certainly singled you out, why? And what did she mean by calling out noble wolf over and over again?"

"On-Gar, I swear I have no idea what that was all about. To be honest, it spooked me. Anyway, yes let's get out of here, did you hear that we will be taking part in a battle tomorrow along with both of Chief Nedrakah's other warbands and yet we have not been told any of this."

On their way back to their own settlement, Ro-Gan and On-Gar saw Orsk chief Snag-Roth.

"Chief, it is good to see you, but can we talk?" asked Ro-Gan.

"Umm, did you do something you shouldn't have, Ro-Gan?"

"No, nothing like that, Chief, no, but we did learn that tomorrow we will be involved in a battle, but I know nothing of this, and I should be preparing my warriors."

The orc laughed. "You should be, yes, but others think that it's better that you and your warriors are not prepared!"

Ro-Gan and On-Gar exchanged puzzled glances. "I don't understand, Chief?"

"Think about it this way, you are the first Hu-man ever to lead a warband, you showed great skill and courage and have a thoughtful mind, both the other war chiefs are of a higher status and are half-breeds and they have been greatly shamed by you both, in combat and in other areas so, why would they want to give you any time to be prepared?"

"What! But surely if we fail and the attackers actually win, then isn't that worse for us all."

"Some fates are worse than death, we are Orsk and half-breeds, you should be nothing more than a slave, as it is you are not, but what great things lay in store other than to be trampled on by those who hold the reins of power?" Chief Snag-Roth shook his head and fell silent and was still shaking his head as he walked away. "Get some sleep, Ro-Gan, and you too, On-Gar, who knows tomorrow you might find yourself in the afterlife picking crud from between the toes of the gods!" Snag-Roth laughed as he went about his way.

"On-Gar, we need to do something this is stupid, and I for one have no intention of sacrificing my life to make anyone

60

else look good or to pick bits from between the toes of the gods!"

"Was Snag-Roth serious, about the toes of the gods I mean?"

"Don't be so ridiculous, On-Gar, the gods love us and secretly so does Snag-Roth."

"Whatever, Ro-Gan, but we will not win any friends either with the gods or the other warbands."

"We are not here to win friends, but I do take it personally when the lives of my warriors are at stake."

All night, Ro-Gan put his charges through their paces, he taught them shield wall tactics just as he remembered from his years with the strange man in his dreams, he had a bad feeling about all of this and he just wanted to get through it with the minimum loss of men and half-orcs.

Brenn and Willem both wanted to join the fight but Ro-Gan refused their request. They might have had experience in their militia but this battle might be against their own people, Ro-Gan's, no, would very definitely mean, no, this time. However, they were allowed to train late into the night with the warband as they also had knowledge of shield wall and other combat tactics.

The following morning, Chief Snag-Roth came around later than usual to rouse the warband.

"Get up, you mangey dogs, get up you have a battle to fight!" Snag-Roth bellowed at the weary warriors of Ro-Gan's warband.

"Chief, if this was the first, we were to hear about this battle then it is a pile of dung!" Ro-Gan certainly made his feeling known to the chief.

"Did you think I would bring breakfast as well, hmm, I am sorry to disappoint, now get dressed everyone is outside waiting!" Snag-Roth was in a belligerent mood, war was a serious business.

As Ro-Gan and his warriors strode out of the tunnels and into the morning light many found themselves shielding their eyes even though at this time the sun was behind them.

Half-breed, Chief Lug-Ran was the first to catch sight of Ro-Gan's straggling warband.

"Good of you to join us, Hu-man, I hope you got a good night's sleep and are refreshed and ready for the battle."

"We are good and ready, lead the way, lord and master!" It was all that Ro-Gan could say, anything else he kept to himself other he thought they wouldn't even make it as far as the battle.

"Do you wish for us to follow your lead or have you made other plans, Lord Chief?"

"We have been informed that a Thegn is coming this way from over the border with Lōrnicā, with his army that at our spotters best guess is at least one hundred strong, they seem to think that we will either give them their money back or honour our agreement to return their two captured children!"

Ro-Gan turned to On-Gar and whispered, "Now how on earth do they know that those boys are here, I wonder?"

On-Gar was equally quiet in his reply. "This stink's worse than Lug-Ran's arm pits!"

Chief Lug-Ran raised his right arm into the early morning air and shouted, "On wards!"

All three warbands broke into an immediate canter while keeping their respective shapes alongside each other.

Coming with the sun behind them meant that the army of Lōrnicā would be surprised by their sudden appearance but even more so because they might be thinking that orcs can't be outside in the daylight, even so Ro-Gan had a feeling deep down in his gut that that this day was really about some other purpose, but what that was, escaped him for the time being.

As the two armies came within a couple of hundred yards of each other, they deployed in formation, those from Lōrnicā, resplendent in green dyed woollen tunics with chainmail shirts, five-foot round shields and eight-foot spears. They formed up thirty men wide three rows deep with shields interlocked.

The three warbands were in an ad hoc formation within their three individual formations and without another word, all three warbands were ordered to charge, Chief Lug-Ran gave the command even though he must have known that this attack would be smashed to pieces on the shield wall in front of them.

Some of the humans threw javelins from the rear rank over their own soldiers and they hit with steely precision taking out around fifteen warriors across the front of the charging warband. Some of the warband returned fire by throwing axes and short spears of their own but most hit harmlessly into the shield wall.

When the two groups clashed together, the warbands were almost immediately repulsed, fight as hard as they might they just could not break through the human's front line, Ro-Gan knew it would be a disaster if they fought this way for much longer but he was reluctant to do anything else while Lug-Ran was in command.

On-Gar offered some encouraging words when he said that soon the humans would tire and then the strength of the warbands would start show, but Ro-Gan was not convinced and so he began to think of a strategy.

After what seemed like hours, but was in fact only minutes, it appeared that Lug-Ran's centre warband was beginning to cave in as more than half his warriors were dead or lay dying in the grass. The humans saw what was about to happen in the centre of the orcs line and the whole of the third row of their army bunched up behind their own centre as reinforcements, for what looked like a final push to break the Orsk.

Lug-Ran took a blow to his sword arm which went limp and fell uselessly to his side and he only saved himself from certain death by bringing his shield up quickly to hammer his enemy's sword out of the way, but then he took another blow to his exposed left leg and this time he went down on one knee as what was left of his centre warband rallied around him. This was the moment Ro-Gan cried out to his warriors, "Shield wall on me!" And all of his remaining fighters locked their shields and pushed back at the two thin rows of humans in front of them.

Ro-Gan had drilled his warriors for hours the previous night and that was beginning to pay off now as his flank began to turn the humans in on itself. More of the humans were starting to charge into the middle by now thinking perhaps that they had already won but instead it just added to the weakening of both their left and right flanks. The second warband that fought on the right was equalling beginning to take advantage of the thinning ranks before them, but they had

64

already lost their own cohesion and both wings were involved in one mass brawl.

Ro-Gan's warband had by now completely turned the left flank of the humans and was pressing home utilising his unit's fearsome strength, those humans suddenly found themselves fighting not only the withering centre but on their left side as well, and as suddenly as that, the humans themselves broke in to a writhing mass of bodies fighting on all sides and some even turned and ran from the battle altogether.

By the time the sun was high in the midday sky, the battle was over with over seventy humans lying dead or dying, as for the warbands, only a badly wounded Lug-Ran and five of his warriors survived, along with eight more from the other warband belonging to Bal-Dok, and sixteen from Ro-Gan's warband.

On-Gar wanted to chase after the humans who by now were throwing anything away that would weight down their escape, armour, weapons, shields and helmets littered the route away from the main battle and the humans were utterly defeated. The rest of the day was taken up with collecting all of the equipment that lay strewn across the battle field and then by savaging for fire wood to make funeral pyres and piling the dead bodies up and setting them alight, any wounded were also thrown unceremoniously into the hungry flames, causing many of those wounded to scream and beg for mercy.

By the night fall, the wild animals of the area came to feast on anything that was left, drawn by the smell of the blood-soaked field. Many of the Orsk were then able to come out of the caves and tunnels and take stock of the battle site and it was at this point that many of those present stopped what they were doing as a large white creature came bounding across the field howling and with its fearsome fangs bared. Smoke from the burning pyres mixed with the cold night air and danced and swirled as the oncoming beast glided through the air effortlessly between leaps.

Some of the Orsk and those who survived the battle just dropped everything and turned towards the safety of the distant tunnels and ran, as if the wild creature the size of a small horse was running after them personally.

Ro-Gan saw that the Chief, Lug-Ran, was left unattended and badly wounded his bodyguard, as they also were in full flight, but Ro-Gan's first instinct was to protect a stricken comrade, nothing more, and so he ran towards the chief, On-Gar shouted a warning, "Look out!" When the creature, fangs and claws out, was almost on the fallen half-breed leader.

However, it was Ro-Gan who arrived first and with just a split second to turn his whole body, shield on arm to cover both himself and the left side of Lug-Ran's crumpled body. The white creature smashed into Ro-Gan's shield with such force it shattered the ash and iron construction into several pieces. With his right hand, Ro-Gan dug his spear into the wet sticky earth and such was the force of the creature's lunge that it drove its self-deep on to the bladed weapon, slicing its open from just under its chin right down to it back legs, and then the spear snapped and the creature landed with a thud on top of both Ro-Gan and the badly wounded orc lord.

On-Gar cried in disappear, transfixed by the sight of blood suddenly explode from everywhere and the creature flatten itself on top of both Ro-Gan and Lug-Ran. There was nothing to be seen except a small white island in a sea of scarlet red. Now all those who had ran began to return tentatively back to the rows of dead bodies, they came in utter astonishment at what they had just witnessed, but there was not a one amongst them who were brave enough to get that close in case the creature was stunned and not dead.

Lord Chief Nedrakah arrived after about half an hour accompanied by the female Orsk, shaman Berba-Shin, she was screaming at the top of her voice, Aatu, Aatu, over and over again, whatever was unfolding was completely incomprehensible to any but herself.

Chief Nedrakah shouted at On-Gar and some of his warriors to pull the creature off the two stricken bodies and they just stood and looked, not even knowing where one body began and another ended. They had to be commanded twice more before they did dare to push their hands into that sea of blood and guts, but as they pulled at the body of the creature, they all recoiled in horror, because there was something stirring deep within the creature's abdomen. Berba-Shin now pushed her way forward once again shouting, "Aatu!"

Without fear or thought for her own safety, the wizened old female orc plunged both her arms in deeper than any of the warrior did and she dragged from the creatures inhered a tiny blood-soaked version of the dead creature, and began to yelp, and just as soon as it was pulled free Berba-Shin started to nuzzle it with her face, and no longer shouting but whispering the word 'Aatu' over and over again. She didn't seem to care that her face was rubbed red with the hot sticky blood of this small things mother.

Chief Nedrakah again issued the order to pull the creatures body clear of their two fallen warriors, once more, and as On-Gar and several others did so, to everyone's amazement both warriors were alive and began gasping for air.

The following day after everybody had washed down and slept for some hours, Ro-Gan, On-Gar and the two other warband chief's, Bal-Dok and Lug-Ran were all called upstairs to a meeting with the orc Warlord Poda-Gog. Already present in the meeting room was the female shaman Berba-Shin, still blood stained and smelling for more fouler than she ever had, and clutching the small creature from the night before, like her life depended on her holding it, but it was no longer red, someone, probably the old Orsk, had washed the blood off its coat, and here it was pure white like the driven snow, and it was treated with such reverence.

The creature had the appeared of a wolf cub, but with one other strikingly distinctive feature, one blue eye and one that was green. Those in the know already guested that it was a white warg welp and Warlord Poda-Gog wanted to keep it as his own personal property, and he reached over to relieve the Shaman of her burden, and she reluctantly allowed it to be taken.

White wargs are a once in a generation anomaly, an Oman of immense power and prestige especially in the Orsk world, and with the edition of eyes that were different colours this minuscule bundle was considered to be token, a familiar from the gods, the most valuable possession one could ever own, if indeed one could even own a token from the gods.

Ro-Gan waited until everyone was seated before he began to speak.

"Silence!" bellowed Warlord Poda-Gog, causing the buddle of white fur held tightly on his lap to jump up and yelp.

"You do not have the right to speak at a council of chief's, Hu-man, your rank does not even give you the right to lick my boots, you who have caused our great cause to be set back years!"

Ro-Gan stared silently in disbelief.

"Chief Lug-Ran, are you well enough to speak?" asked the Warlord.

"Yes, Lord Poda-Gog, I am stunned in my right arm, and I have a wound on my left leg otherwise I am, I will be perfectly fine?"

"Then you will speak, now, so that we can all see what went wrong yesterday?"

One or two of the other high-ranking Orsk began to bang the tabletop with fists.

"That coward, Ro-Gan, and his warband hid behind their shields when I shouted to charge the battle plan would have proceeded perfectly if he had just followed that order," Lug-Ran recalled.

"Chief Bal-Dok, is this account exactly as you saw it?"

"Yes, Lord Chief. Chief Lug-Ran and I were executing your plan perfectly until this filthy creature's cowardice."

"Berba-Shin, it would seem that not even your intervention can keep this wretched Hu-man alive much longer, what say you, Shaman?"

"I say let not I speak, but let the God speak for us!" The old hag cackled.

"What are you babbling about foolish women, you are only here because you are the last of the true Orsk shaman, but you have already been out manoeuvred."

Just at that moment, Berba-Shin burst into the ancient tongue of the Orsk, the black dialect of ancient times, they language of the gods, that should never be spoken in front of any other than the goddess of blood herself.

"Sandraudiga, she who dyes the land red, I implore you to speak to this council today, tell us what we must do!"

Silence befell the room.

For some time, only the yapping of the white warg pup was heard until Berba-Shin broke the mood and silence by asking the warlord why he held on to the pup so tightly.

Warlord Poda-Gog let go of the warg, in fact so confident of the pup staying with him he raised both arms above his head and smiled at the orc woman, the pup turned a couple of times on Poda-Gog's lap before it promptly cocked it's leg up and pee'd up Poda-Gog's tunic. Poda-Gog roared at the tiny white bundle, and the creature yelped one more time and then jumped off his lap, and under the table that separated each of the individuals from one another.

The pup went straight to the feet of Ro-Gan and began sniffing his boots it's tiny white tail wagging furiously, then it looked up just once with those piercing eyes and jumped on Ro-Gan's knee.

"The gods have spoken, Lord Chief!" the old, wizened Orsk spat the words out daring any to challenge what she had just said.

Lug-Ran clenched the arm of his chair his face twisted in anguish.

Bal-Doc was about to speak when Poda-Gog slammed his fists hard down on the tabletop, this was not the outcome he had wanted nor could he over turn what appeared to be the will of the God's.

"Leave me, now all of you!" Poda-Gog bellowed. However, as Ro-Gan held the pup with his right hand to then raise from his seat Poda-Gog held out his hand.

"Stay, Ro-Gan, we have things still to discuss."

Ro-Gan returned to his seated position and released his hold on the pup, to which the pup stretched up to lick Ro-Gan vigorous about his chin and face.

Poda-Gog saw this display of affection and his heart sank, the gods had truly spoken and all the warlords plans now hung in the balance.

"What would you have me do next, Ro-Gan, or perhaps I should ask your new pet?"

"Lord Chief, I am but your humble servant, I have a warband to tend to and I wish only to await on your new instructions, that is all."

"You are a stupid insubordinate, Hu-man, who cannot follow orders and whose stupidity will put an end to everything we do here in the kingdom under the mountain, alas. It is the will of the gods that you are right, and I am wrong, go now to your precious warband and lick your wounds. I will deliberate on these matters and give my verdict in the morning. Now leave me and take your pet with you, GO!"

The settlement of Nedrakah slept a very uneasy sleep that night although one warband remained largely intact the other two warbands or what was left of them plotted and schemed the death of the usurper, Ro-Gan. For his part in all of this, Ro-Gan was content, but the visions in his mind as he tossed and turned had returned and they became to him like a curse, in the form of hot and cold sweats.

Before the evening ended for Poda-Gog too would find his sleep would not be a peaceful one, because one more visitor was abroad and prowling the upper corridors and passageways, and that night and he let himself in to the chamber of the warlord.

"Who dares to disturb Centurion Vagun-Gad, what brings you so far down in to the belly of the mountain."

"You have caused us all a great deal of dissatisfaction, Poda-Gog, and I have been sent to gain some assurances that all is not as it seems."

"Perhaps we underestimated our faithful half-breeds and a single human as out witted them?" Poda-Gog was having a personal dig at the Centurion who was himself a half-breed under all his armour.

"Perhaps we have underestimated you, Poda-Gog, and we should swap your place with Lug-Ran?"

"Lug-Ran is a fool, his mission was only to scare the men of Lōrnicā, dead men after all do not pay their way."

"We all saw what happened, we watched from the hillside, your Hu-man made a plan of his own and killed all but a few of the men from Lōrnicā, he made the two half-breed leaders look stupid and incompetent, the Hu-mans might think that we are weak and that they don't need to invest in our mercenaries to keep them safe at night."

"They don't need your help, Centurion, they have not been convinced by your tricks surely that is what you mean, so you come down here and try to lay all of the blame on me, well go ahead I have lived longer than anyone expected and I am not afraid to embrace my ancestors!"

"The half-breeds who fail their initiation in to the black guard are left with you for a reason, and if that reason is purely to die, surely then their death in combat, is a sacrifice to our God's and a surety that our wider plans will work out, Orsk are a dying breed and you have been for years Poda-Gog, hidden away in your caves not able to come out in the daylight, we are the future of Orsk kind!"

"Nevertheless, as I said you cannot hope to achieve anything with your precious half-breeds unless we, the true blood Orsk, help you!"

"Then rid yourself of all these Hu-mans and the useless half-breeds that would bring us all to ruin and we will start the program anew, in this settlement, do I make myself understood?"

"Yes, Centurion, fully!"

At first light the following morning, all of the humans and the half-breeds were assembled in the large cave, along with all the survivors from the other two warbands. The balcony area filled with many of the Orsk chiefs from different settlement for miles around under the mountains.

Chief Snag-Roth was the one who raised his hands for silence and began to speak.

"There is but one rule here in Nedrakah and that one rule is to obey orders, if you cannot obey orders, you will begin to question our purpose, and then everything will fall apart."

Voices were heard agreeing with what was said but those voices came from the balcony and those below in the arena stayed silent.

"Lug-Ran, you failed your orders. Guards, take out this traitor!"

"Bal-Dok you failed your orders also, your failures must be taken care of, guards!"

Several Orsk guards shuffled forward so they stood in two groups around the half-breed chiefs.

"Kill them both!" roared chief Snag-Roth.

"Ro-Gan, you will take charge of all of their surviving warriors you may even take their gold and silver bracelets, but know this Ro-Gan you also failed to obey orders but with hindsight your victory brought unexpected benefits, now the Hu-mans are truly scared of us and they will pay even more for our protection, your insubordination though cannot go unpunished"

The white warg pup began to yelp and the Orsk in the upper balcony began to murmur.

Berba-Shin saw her opportunity and stepped forward to speak. "The gods have had their payment in blood, and they are grateful, but be careful that they do not want an over payment." Berba-Shin did not want Ro-Gan or his pup to be killed, they had to survive this purge, she had seen his timeline continue and above all else, the will of the God's would not be mocked!

Now it was Warlord Poda-Gog's turn to step forward and speak, barely able to contain his anger, he spat out his words with venom, "Enough! Ro-Gan and all of you warriors are henceforth banished from this land and you are to empty the chambers where the captive women stay, go now and clean this place of your stench before I call the Black Guard to do it for you!"

4 A New Beginning

Sixty four weary men, women and half-breeds along with half as many children, again, were frog marched unceremoniously by armed Orsk guards to the front of the tunnel that which would take them out in to the chilly Aragus morning, it was autumn and the mornings were exceptionally light but the sun was not high enough to warm the land.

They had each been allowed to take just a few days dry rations, for the thirty three league journey, and some water in a small animal skin, one that was usually given to weening children, and they must have all been apprehensive at the thought of leaving with such little food, but Snag-Roth approached Ro-Gan quietly and without drawing attention to them, and he said in a low voice, "Remember your training, out on the hunt, and walk in the straightest possible line keeping the sun to your left until mid-day and then to your left until the moon comes out."

The view was breath-taking at first, the slope from the base of the mountain, ran slightly down hill and the grass was lush and in several shades of green, interposed with patches of brown where wild animals had spent hours eating the grass. There was not a single tree insight in any direction and neither were there any hedge rows of bushes, the landscape was barren except for the grass.

It was blustery because it was exposed but it was freezing bit then nor was it that warm, Rogan though about the small children and whether they would be able to keep warm enough, especially as it got very cold at night and they had been allowed to bring just one skin blanket with each, and they had nothing else to keep them warm other than the clothes on their backs.

It was Rogan's wish at first that they all pick up the pace as he was worried that the Orsk would renege on their agreement to let everyone from the cave village of Nedrakah go free, but he also knew that as savage and barbaric as they were they still had their own warped sense of duty and codes with which to live by. The Orsk were also under guidance from Berba-Shin, the Orsk shaman, and they would not dare to have crossed their gods.

Right from the beginning, Ro-Gan realised that food would not actually be a problem as the whole area was covered in sea birds and small animals could be seen darting about between the birds' nesting areas. Where the problem might arise was from Ro-Gan insisting that no campfires were to be lit, not while they were still so close to the kingdom under the mountain, and he reminded them that the Orsk could run at night much faster than they were travelling during the day.

After three weary days of walking, Ro-Gan began to ease up on everyone. He knew they were hungry for hot food and that there were only so many fresh eggs that could be eaten by sucking the contents out cold through a tiny hole. Fatigue and exhaustion would be the real enemy not the Orsk, if they had made no attempt to catch them by now then they never would.

So, on the morning of the fourth day, Ro-Gan let them stop and prepare small cooking fires and fashion shelters from anything they could find washed up on the beach. From this day onwards, they stopped each morning at first light for one hour and cooked food for the day, some of that time was taken trying to catch the many small birds that nested there, because freshly cooked meat was an important meal for them all, after the break was over, then they walked until last light and stopped again for another hour and hot food.

At some point, they came across more of the rough wooden posts that it appeared had once been a border boundary between Obreā and the neighbouring realm of Lōrnicā. Both Brenn and Willem had recognised them from the time that they spent in the militia, patrolling up and down this very area but on the other side of the posts, and they said that if these posts were followed, they would lead directly to the neck of the river Tawa, that river formed part of the boundary between, Obreā, Lōrnicā, and Fōrren.

There was a freshwater stream that appeared out of the ground where some of the posts were placed and this, Brenn said becomes a brook that leads into the Tawa. Rogan used this opportunity for everyone to stop and refill their animal skins, and to take a bite from their dried meat rations.

Sadly, at this point, it was discovered that three of the babies had died, from what nobody knew, two of them were human and one was a half-blood. Both the human babies were very tiny and came early in their mother's pregnancy, however the half-blood was a female, the first that Rogan had even heard of and the mother swore him to secrecy as she had seen the birth as an ill Oman.

Rogan did not breach that trust with the mother although he had become curious about baby girls that must have been born as half-bloods, On-Gar laughed at him saying there were no such thing, and that it was silly even thinking such a thing. Although it made perfect sense to Rogan, but it looked like it was another question to be answered at another time, and so he forgot about the question but felt both sorrow and guilt for the mother.

It was about this time that some of the people started to ask why they didn't just cross this flimsy boarder and just give themselves up to the people of Lōrnicā, surely, they would welcome Brenn and Willem back with open arms, to which the boys didn't disagree, but they pointed out that the half-bloods would not be made welcome, and in fact may find themselves imprisoned all over again.

The journey to the neck of the river Tawa would take another three days and it was noticeable that it was the border point between the three realms because it was where the brook led into a larger river and that larger river joined the Tawa. Brenn advised that they cross the brook into Lōrnicā and then quickly cross the river, which was wide enough for boats and certainly deep enough for them, but then cross that into Fōrren, it would be easier than trying to cross the neck of the Tawa here because it was still too wide and too deep.

Ro-Gan, at this point began to think about his old geography teacher, a monk whose name escaped him, they were all either monks or father this or brother that, anyway, this particular one had taught him where he was in the grand scheme of things, which meant that Mārcādiā was at the centre of it all, Rogan thought that the name might even be something to do with it literally being in the middle, but it also showed where all the other realms and places where around them. The more he thought about it, the more it came back to him, there was a huge map of the Shattered Realms on the wall behind where the monk would sit.

The river was too deep for everyone to get across safely especially those who were carrying things like babies, so Rogan said that he would swim across and go and look for a safer way to bring the rest across, and so they should camp here at least until he returned, and so as he began to strip his clothes off down to his under garments, he called out the names of Gun-Nar, At-Li, Dri-Gar, Bren-Mir and finally Brenn, they were to come with him across the river, and so they too began to strip down.

The group had brought their clothes wrapped tightly in to rolls and an axe each, in case they came across a smallish tree or some other wood that could be chopped into similar sizes and shapes that could be lashed together to make a raft, a raft would keep the babies from drowning and some of the other stuff from getting soaked. When they unravelled, their clothes to their amazement only the outer garment was wet the others had stayed relatively dry.

They followed the course of the river Tawa until they came across what looked like a small building sat back just a little way from the water, it was wooden and on four rough stone legs and had a turf roof, there was no smoke from the chimney which indicated that no one was home, or that they had fallen asleep, either way Ro-Gan told the others to be as quite as they could while staying alert to any dangers.

The small building was in fact someone's home, but that might have been a while ago, such things as heavily cobwebbed windows and tall brush grass growing over the lintel of the door, and the lack of a fire of course, gave evidence of that. Rogan slowly eased the front door off its latch and pushed it open, the door hinges squealed in response to this action which was another indicator that the occupier was long gone.

The other boys had spread out to look around the back and the sides of the building and Bren-Mir, the half-blood had gone to look both ways down the river. The air inside the building was musty and as the rays from the sun found their way in through the open door and cracks in the shuttered windows Rogan could see tiny dust clouds swirling around as though they were stung by the light and thirsted only for the darkness, it made Rogan shudder but he could see the place was sound, but abandoned.

Everybody was alerted to a call from Bren-Mir by the river, it was just low enough as not to be heard far away, but loud enough to state, to the others, that he had found something of interest. When they all met outside the front door and looked to where Bren-Mir had been, they saw him waving, beckoning them to where he was, and so they jogged over their not thinking it was anything too serious as he had a big silly grin on his face.

They were a boat, a small two, three, or four, man boat tied to a mooring post in the embankment at the river's edge, "By the one true God!" said Ro-Gan.

"I didn't know that you believed in the one true God, Ro-Gan?" Gun-Nar quipped.

"I guess I do more when things like this happen, a boat is more than I could have hoped for, lets row back to the others, get them on this side of the river and bring them to the house, it will make a good place to hold up at least until we can figure out our next move."

It was decided that they would stay at the house at least for the nigh and almost immediately a group of the women began to tidy the place up, while Rogan had sent a couple of search parties out for food and to spy out the land, Brenn had said that this northern part of Fōrren would be sparsely populated but the people from around here were thought of as being hostile to any outsiders and even gave the traders a hard time coming both ways in and out of Fōrren to trade their wares in Lōrnicā.

"Use only dry wood for the fire, brake up a table or chair if you have too, because I don't want anyone nearby snooping on us, understood?"

They all nodded in acknowledgement. Recalling minding the map on the wall of his old school house, if they continued to follow the river Tawa, then they would eventually come out in Mārcādiā, a thought that made him shudder involuntarily, not because of any thoughts of animosity towards that realm, but because the very thought invoked bad memories, he suddenly had a feeling that it was somewhere near there that he was snatched all those years ago.

At-Li asked what other options they had.

Rogan suggested that the further down country they go the more densely populated it will be and they all still have green dyed skin and there were quite a lot of them, and Aatu although still a very small pup was apt to howl at people he didn't know, which could again, draw unwanted attention to them, the larger towns and villages comigrated further south in Fōrren.

Ro-Gan offered a better solution, that they cross the river here and make their way into Råvenniå, that was a massive realm with plenty of wide-open space in the north. Besides which as they looked out across the river they saw only dense wooded forest, and no signs of civilisation. Snag-Roth had even revealed to Ro-Gan that many years ago the Orsk would trade with some of those northern villages for things like oil, and something he called whale bone.

Bren and Willem both added that those times were long past, that would have been before the Kristosiān's came and conquered the land, they had tried to reunite the realms, in order to fulfil a prophecy about somewhere his father called the Re-United Kingdoms, but they agreed that there was land enough. "You could lose a whole realm like Lōrnicā in the space that was Northern Råvenniå," Willem chipped in.

Using the small boat, first to transport all of their equipment across the river, and then to take the women and babies and small children, all of the rest of the menfolk and a number of the women, decided it would help if they all swam across. Once on the other side, those who needed got themselves dressed and the women and children arranged themselves for the next part of their journey, across the open plains towards a large forest towards the east.

Walking into the mid-day sun was not ideal, and once again Rogan was reminded of the times, he had fallen foul of not being able to see what was a head of him, but he argued on this occasion there were really nothing that he could have done about it, it was what it was, and it was while he had been day dreaming that On-Gar began pointing excitedly, saying, "Look, it is smoke!"

There was a whisp from somewhere either on the other side of the forest or right in the middle of it. Either way there was still some distance to cover before they reached the outer edges and could reassess from there. Some of the others had noticed that this open expanse contained a large variety of animals, one of which was a large hairy cow looking creature that was a reddish brown in colour, there were massive herds of them just lazily eating the grass.

The plant life had changed as well, now there was a wavy hair-grass; its fine, hair-like leaves and delicate pink flower heads could be seen shaking in the gentle breeze, then there was soft, downy looking plant that was white like fog that looked like it was a favourite of caterpillars and of the Small winsome butterfly's.

Golden-brown reedbeds formed by stands of Common reed that announced the presence of wetlands, and the fluffy, white heads of common cotton-grass, and the distinctive spiky, or green flower heads of wild barley that the children would pick and throw at each other like little arrow heads that stuck on their Woolley outer garments, it was good to hear the cheerful cries of the children, and for the first time in quite a while the adults had a real sense of hope.

Now, as the forest came closer into view the tall trees acted as a partial shade to the eyes, and the enormity of the woodland area came into view, it was probably the size of the kingdom under the mountain alone. Alder was the first recognisable tree to be seen in any great numbers as it grew around the wetland areas, but there was Ash, much loved by weaponsmiths and Aspen whose leaves and branches

83

trembled and fluttered again in the gentlest of breezes, and many others besides.

Then it was the smell of burning wood, but not that the wood was on fire but that someone somewhere had built for themselves a camp fire, and even the aroma of slowly cooking meat was detectable, and so it was decided, the people would camp on the edge of the forest while Ro-Gan and some of his men would try to go deeper in to the woods and follow the trial of smoke, Aatu seemed restless at the thought of being left behind and so as the small group walked away. He decided that he would follow.

Gun-Nar was left in charge while Ro-Gan took the two new boys, Brenn and Willem, On-Gar, Ingrid and of course Aatu, who was struggling to be seen over the height of the tall grass. Although it was nearly impossible to see the sun Ro-Gan when he caught sight determined that it was well past mid-day and they were getting tired which meant that they must have walked for a good two or three hours, but instead of seeing anyone, their first contact would be by sound.

There was the sound of men talking, laughing and joking in a dialect that Ro-Gan had a bit of trouble completely understanding at first, because the trees formed a natural barrier and there was the constant 'thunk' of metal on wood. Ro-Gan signalled for caution and the group crouched as they walked forwards, Aatu wasn't so stealthy, he struggled to walk at all and found it much more fun to leap and jump about, so that they were overtly aware of the snap and crackle as he kept up with them.

When the first sighting of the men in the forest took place, it could be seen that they dressed in linen cloth which was dyed predominately brown, a fairly common dye derived from walnut shells, and the odd splash of yellow, again not an uncommon colour that is mixed using weld, turmeric, saffron, and onion skins, all this told Ro-Gan that these wood cutters were ordinary folk, there wasn't a piece of armour nor a proper weapon in sight.

The woodsmen were observed selecting various trees to be chopped down and each was armed with large two-handed axes, while others hitched horses to the fallen trunks and dragged them away further away through the clearing that they had made, and something else Ro-Gan noticed was the lack of a good road or even a visible track, these men were making their own, so they knew this forest like the back of their hands.

One of the wood cutters reacted when he heard what was an unusual sound to his ears, it was of course the playful yapping of a baby warg that was being ignored by its master. The alerted woodsman signalled to the rest of the men to be quiet. "Whose be hiding, come out now less you be lawless robbers!" he spoke without knowing where Ro-Gan was hiding but he clutched his axe tightly and he girded his loins ready for a surprise assault.

Ro-Gan, cover blown, stepped out into the clearing and raised his hands, Brenn, Willem, On-Gar, and Ingrid followed suit, and Aatu continued to dance around Ro-Gan's feet leaping and yapping excitedly. "Halt, ye!" shouted the woodman who first became aware of their presence.

"Place yer' weapons slowly on the ground and no sudden movements!"

Ro-Gan first held his sword high over his head with his right hand, then he nodded to demonstrate that he understood, and then he crouched and placed the weapon on the ground, the others did the same, and Aatu took this opportunity to jump up breathlessly and lick Ro-Gan's face.

"Friend! We come in peace," Ro-Gan said, trying to keep his words simple and clear to prevent any misunderstanding.

There were six of the woodsmen each holding the axes and looking directly at him with wide eyed wonder, and then at Brenn and Willem who were at least a hand small than the others, then On-Gar who exuded muscle and finally at the women. After they had seemed to drink in the vision of mystery that stood before them, one of the woodcutters plucked up the courage to speak.

"Who are ye, and why doth ye, be seeking to sneak up on us, is this villainy on yer part?" asked the woodmen, visibly tightening his grip on his axe.

Ro-Gan was now unarmed except for a dagger that rested in his belt across his waist. "My name is Ro-Gan and these are my kin, and this here is my, er, pet dog, we are travellers looking for a sanctuary to settle and we come in peace. As you can see from my dog, we are cautious, yes. But not trying to conceal ourselves or our intentions."

"Yer skin has a greenish hue and so you are of Orsk stock, except for the girl, and you all stink like pigs that have wallowed too long in their own excrement, why is this?"

"Is the girl yer prisoner, by any chance, and you have come to sell her to us as slave, is that yer real intention, stranger?"

"No, no, the girl is free to come and go, you see our settlement was raided by Orsk many days ago, our village is far to the north, and this, this is a disguise, we covered ourselves in green dye, to look like Orsk and we have been on the run and hiding out from them ever since."

"If ye be refugees as ye say ye are, where are the rest of your kinfolk, or was your village tiny, so tiny in fact that it as if it wasn't even there?

"We followed the trail of your smoke and set up a camp at the west of us, there we have settled our kinfolk until we could make contact."

"How many kinfolks do yer have?" asked another of the woodcutters.

"We number, sixty-four adult men and women and about half as many children and babies."

"How many of you are true warriors?" the first man asked, who looking at On-Gar as he spoke.

"About thirty-two, but as you can plainly see, we are all young and have little or no practice at warcraft."

"So, if you are not warriors, then what may I ask is your trade, for you are fine looking young men, and women, and I certainly would not hesitate to stand with you in a shield wall?"

The latest speaker was a well build square shouldered man who was seen to wield his axe with style and purpose, and if his appearance was any indication of his status, then he was a decorated warrior. Standing at almost eighteen hands high (six feet), with his hair shaved off at the sides and sleeked back into a plated ponytail, either side of his remaining hair his scalp was tattooed with patterns of scrolls and swirls.

"All of us menfolk are trained blacksmiths, the women are seamstresses and mothers."

"Blacksmiths! You are a village of blacksmiths, that certainly would explain your muscles, but tell me stranger from the far north, who were you shaping your metal for, I may be a simple woodsman but I am not a complete fool, no body lives beyond our village, that land beyond belongs to the Orsk, and our village is still a league or more south of here?"

Ro-Gan hesitated, to lie did not sit well with him, but to tell the truth gave him a sinking feeling deep in his stomach.

"Speak!" demanded the man. "And mind your words, I might have welcomed you more freely if you had told me that you were part of a band of travelling entertainers!"

Ro-Gan felt his heart sink and he turned to his younger companion with tears in his eyes, and with a sense of resignation.

"We were all captives of the Orsk, the menfolk did train as both warriors and blacksmiths, and it was the Orsk who made them all wash in green dye, the women folk and I were, to our eternal shame, were kept as concubines against our will and locked in chains day and night," Ingrid said with conviction.

"If this is true, then my lady please except my apology if I have been harsh with my words, so must be from Obreā! Does this mean that the Orsk under the mountain, are chasing you, if I help you will I be putting my village in danger?"

"We were made free by the Orsk at the request of the hag Berba-Shin, she said that the gods demanded it after we, the warriors, had been of concern to them. In the days that we have been travelling, we have not seen any signs that they might be following us. but know this we have fought them once and have prevailed, so I am sure that they will not bother us again."

"Then let us open up our stores to you and your people, come be my guest, bring all of your people to our village, it is about one nights walk away, you can spend the rest of the day there but then I think it is better that you continue with your journey, do you understand?"

"Yes, and thank you, my lord, to help repay your generosity. I would ask that you cut down twice as many trees and when my people get here, we will help drag them to your village."

The woodcutter turned to his compatriots and waved his arms about himself. "What are we waiting for, come let us chop wood!" Then he turned back towards Ro-Gan and introduced himself.

"My name is Gufi Grettersson and I am the chieftain of Hundsnes, these are a few of my most trusted men. My second, Brogan Ebonwulf and the little one is my son Ahlaege."

"My name, my lord is, Ro-Gan and these are my trusted companions, On-Gar, Brenn, Willem, Ingrid and my pet dog, Aatu."

"If you don't mind me asking, On-Gar is not a human, is he?"

"He is called by the Orsk, a half-breed, but we call him half-blood."

"He is not Orsk, then what is he, this half-blood?"

"He is the child of a union between Orsk and human."

When the rest of Ro-Gan's people arrived at the camp where the wood cutters had waited it was decided that it would be better if they stayed the night and rested, there were many extra trees that had been felled and Ro-Gan wasn't even sure how they would move them at that point.

The woodsmen suggested that each trunk would need at least six people to pull it at walking pace, but that had a method that made things a lot easier. "Look, we have cut branches in to rollers, get some of your children to place them in a row in front of the trunk you intend to pull, and then once the trunk is pulled over them, start the whole process again, you understand?"

"Yes, I see, your really are nobody's fool, my lord, Grettersson."

"Phew! Call me, Gufi and with talk like that I will have to introduce you to my wife, but she won't have a word of it."

Ro-Gan got up early the next morning and went around to speak to each of the small groups of his people and they began re-lighting the fires that had gone out in the early hours, breakfast would be an important meal especially since they would be hauling ten large trees down a dirt track to a village some leagues away.

Gufi had sent some of his woodsmen out into the forest and they caught a dozen or so rabbits and found some wild mushrooms and root vegetables so that they could make a stew, and everyone ate to their fill before the long pull began to the village of Hundsnes.

As the camp was starting to pack away, the woodsmen began to hook their trees to the horses that they had brought with them, and On-Gar was splitting the people into groups of six fairly evenly balanced individuals. Between them they would move those ten extra trees for the woodsmen that would bring them a lot of extra money for their village.

The journey was not an unpleasant one despite a certain amount of pushing, pulling and groaning, the children seemed to have made a game out of picking up the rollers and running around the front with them to start the whole process off again, and again. Chief Gufi was the only one who wasn't part of a team and he had wandered over to where Ingrid was pulling with all her strength. "Would you like me to take over for a while to give you time to rest?"

"No, it's all right I can manage, but thank you."

As they got nearer and nearer to the village, they could hear the hustle and bustle coming from inside and they caught the smell of many fires cooking many different things, the aroma was pleasant and for the second time, it felt like everything was going to be fine, and then just as suddenly as that there was a clearing in the forest and the tall wooden walls came into view.

Hundsnes was surrounded by thick dense forest on every side, it was an island in a sea of trees, from the edge of the forest to the edge of the village it must have been over three hundred paces, possibly as many as five hundred, the wooden walls were tree trunks that had been knocked into the ground, or buried, Ro-Gan didn't like to ask, and they sat on top of an earthen mound, using soil that had been dug out of a ditch that also ran the circumference of the settlement. Together it must have been the height of three men standing on each other's shoulders.

As the large group came around the front where the two wooden gate towers were, a road could clearly be seen leading in and out of the gates, out was heading south, and the road surface looked as though it were made from crushed stone that had been flattened into what looked like quite a flat surface, and Ro-Gan wondered where the road would lead and what was on the other end of it.

Once inside the village, it was spacious and well set out. There were paths with neat little houses either side and all of the houses were made from wood, and sat on short stubby stone legs, Gufi had said that it was to keep the rats out, not every house was constructed in the same way but a large proportion were made up of cross pieces of wood that over lapped each other and which were attached to a wooden frame, every house had a turf roof, except for one much larger building that sat proudly in the centre of the village, it had a thatched roof and that was where the chief lived.

Gufi asked Ro-Gan and his companions, the ones that he had met personally to come join him at his house, which they later learned was called a lodge, all of the others were taken in by families at the request of the chief, it was only meant to be for one night and although Gufi's people were apprehensive they still welcomed individuals into their respective houses.

The trees that Ro-Gan's people had brought were left at the gates, Brogan Ebonwulf had said that he would arrange for the teams of horses to fetch them over to the saw mills, and the people should go and sample the villagers' hospitality, and so they did just that, however it was soon become apparent that Gufi's people were not so quick to pick the half-bloods to be their guests, so Gufi went around each of his personal body guard and instructed them to take the half-bloods into their family homes.

A feast was prepared and Gufi once more made a fuss of Ingrid by insisting she sat on the opposite side of him around the large table, and on the other side to his own wife, who was a stout looking women with a plain face and good manners, though it might be suspected by those who watched those sorts of things, that she was none too happy with the placement of Ingrid.

While everyone was tucking into their food which consisted of three courses and several different meats from:

pork, chicken and other domestic fowl; beef, Cod and herring had all been prepared and placed out for everyone to enjoy, but there weren't any noticeable vegetables, perhaps they were harder to grow in the forest, thought Ro-Gan.

Gufi enjoyed telling the story of how Hundsnes grew from a simple farm range into the huge village it had become today, the population had only just this year surpassed the five hundred mark, that was the number of residents to officially become a village, anything less and you were living in a settlement, Settlements were allowed to pay taxes by tribute, in other words by bringing food stuffs, produce and the like, where as a village paid in coin.

Gufi could call on the Jarl's army to defend his land in time of attack and he could take advantage of the realms legal people, were as a settlement was largely left to its own devises.

A village could also keep a standing guard of trained men, up to half as many mounted as were on foot, in Hundsnes that equated to a little over eighteen mounted men, thirty-six trained guards and a militia that comprised of around another fifty men. A settlement could only raise a militia.

Ro-Gan could see that Gufi genuinely loved his village and that from the reaction of his people they too had great affection for him, and his family. Ro-Gan then inquired about the beautifully constructed road that led up to the main gates, and Gufi said that he could not lay claim to building that, it was here when this whole place was just a woodland villa, but Rogan had to ask what that meant. He had heard the name, Kristosiān's mentioned before but he had no real understanding about them.

93

Gufi said that he didn't know much but he knew a man who did, and he and shouted for the minstrel who was sat on a stool in the corner of the hall and who was playing a musical instrument, Ro-Gan later learned was called a lyre. Gufi introduced the young man as Aethelric the Bard and said that he was the cleverest man in northern Råvenniå, to which Aethelric just smiled.

Aethelric explained that the Kristosiān's where an ancient race, some thought them giants, however, they were not, they were people just like us, they conquered much of the Shattered Realms and then began to either assimilate the locals in to their culture or just bring in their own, they were master builders and fearsome warriors.

When Aethelric overheard a comment from young Brenn, he quickly picked up on his accent and said, "Young master, am I to assume that you are from Lōrnicā?"

"Yes, I am, why?"

"Because your people still wear very much the same clothes that their forefathers did, your people are distantly related to the Kristosiān's, probably more so than any other race in these realms, it was the furthest north they built, and your capital city was entirely built by them, also, I mean why else would anyone live in such a far-flung place?"

"Hey!"

A great roar of laughter rose up and many began to tease the boy.

"Don't worry I am only joking, Lōrnicā is as beautiful as it is tranquil."

"One of their high-ranking people must have liked this area because they had a villa built here and he must also have had plenty of coin because they built the road as well, a villa

94

was a large complex of buildings with a bath house as well, but these things have long since gone in places like this, sadly."

"Well, for me it is time for sleep, so I will bid you all a good night," said the chief.

5 A Place to Call Home

After everyone had said goodnight to Gufi and his family, except his eldest son, Ahlaege who wanted to stay longer as he was enjoying the camaraderie, Brogan Ebonwulf took over sitting in Gufi's seat, as was the custom in these parts. His first command was to call for more ale for his guests, which brought another round of cheers and laughter.

Brogan continued the story of Hundsnes, from a villa it became a farmstead and then much later a settlement, but now we are a village, that supplies most of the wood to Lāngāholt, Kaldakinn and the town of Ingolfsfell, as you can see, we are a simple folk who live a rich and happy life. A statement that brought yet more cheering and tabletop banging.

Ro-Gan himself was getting tired and he asked where we was to sleep, to which Brogan answered, "Anywhere you wish, the hall is for all of you, so just collect some furs from around the outside walls and make yourselves comfortable, and I shall take that as a hint that I too should turn in for the night, come on Ahlaege, you too."

That night, Rogan and all of his people had probably the most restful night's sleep that they could remember in a very long time, the food had been exceptional, as was the company, and they all got to sleep in warm soft beds of fur, undisturbed the whole night long. The next morning, those in the hall were awaked early by the servants as they began to clear away from the night before in order to prepare for the day ahead.

The chieftain was also a very early riser, and he came to sit around the large open hearth and began sipping mead from a wooden tankard, soon some new faces began to file into the hall, and they too picked up tankards of mead and joined Gufi but around the table and not the fire. "These fine-looking gentlemen are our beloved council Aldermen," the chief said.

Ro-Gan nodded to each in turn and then said a general good morning aimed at everyone present, "I trust you all slept well, and my servants didn't disturb you too much this morning?"

Ro-Gan had said it was probably for the best if they did get up early because they would be leaving soon.

"Tell us all again the story you told me yesterday, please Ro-Gan so that my councillors and I might think together the best way that we could help you."

Ro-Gan then repeated the truth about how they had come to be here, and the Aldermen all listened intently, some from time to time asked for something Ro-Gan had just said to be repeated so that they understood everything and when he had finished, they began to deliberate.

"So, you say that you have nowhere in mind with which you would all like to settle?" asked a councillor.

"Honestly, we just want a place to call home, where we can settle down and raise crops and families and grow old together, all of us, but we want to be productive and we swear to be protective, we could help train warriors and they could help teach us new skills, but I realise that we are many mouths to feed, but we could stay here if you would have us?"

"Why can we not stay here and help you chop wood and protect you from any wandering bandits?" Rogan asked innocently.

"Well, for one, there haven't been any wandering anything's in these woods for generations, and secondly there is nowhere for you to live, unless you think we should just knock down part of our defences and extend our village?"

"Don't lose heart yet though because an idea is formulating in my head, which is still full of all that ale we drank last night, but give it time, anyway, if I could make a suggestion that I think might help going forward, not least because all of your menfolk are still very much green."

"Ah, yes we are, I think I too had too much ale, I thought that I was normal again!"

"Well, anyway, as I was going to say, drop the Orsk sounding names, for example simply change Ro-Gan to Rogan, and get yourselves a last name like mine, I am Grettersson because Gretters was my father's name, in fact everyone in this village is somebodies' son or daughter so their surname ends in son or daughter!"

For a few moments, everyone had a bit of fun stating their new name and shaking hands with the person next to them, it caused a lot of laughter amongst councillors and Rogan's people, and everyone was in merry mood.

On-Gar became, Ongar. Gun-Nar, Gunner. At-Li, Atli, and so on and so forth until every male had a new name, and then came another game, finding a good last name, some remembered their birthing mothers' names and took them but for the half-bloods that was slightly more difficult for many were quickly rejected at birth and so placed with surrogate mothers instead.

"Rogan, have you given any thought to a last name yet?" asked the chieftain.

"I am sorry, Gufi, my head is full of rocks this morning and I can't think of anything!" Rogan replied.

"Then I shall help you, there is no point going one foot outside my village if you only have one name, everybody will be wondering who you are, why you are green, and where you came from, so we need to make you one of us, I think."

"Well, I know I had a life before I was kidnapped but I can't for the life of me remember any names let alone last names, I am sorry, Gufi."

"Hmm, I have got it! And please don't take offense, I name you Rogan Ragisson, in my tongue that means you are Rogan Scarecrow, on account of you looking like a scarecrow!"

"Gufi! I thought we were going to be serious," Rogan blurted out in astonishment.

"No, no, you will see, you are Rogan Ragisson and you are the chieftain of your own displaced people, looking for a new place to call home, you all even look like a ragtag band of wandering scarecrows, look, see you have brought your wives and children with you, it's perfect! And now I think I know the perfect place for you to fit right in."

"I see your point, we are a bit thread bare in these cloths, anyway if you are truly serious, then tell me where is this perfect place you have in mind?"

"All right, that's the spirit, so if you leave here by the main gates that road leads straight down into the valley, but after one league, maybe less there is a left turn, that will take you all the way to the coast. There you will find a small village with a lot of empty houses, it is called Kāldākinn, it is about thirty-four leagues from here which is around nine hours by wagon and horse, all of those I can lend you, of course."

"Thank you, Gufi, but will I ever repay your generosity?"

"Nah! Don't worry, we will work something out I'm sure, anyway, it is very similar to our village in size but it only has a couple of hundred people living there, the main industry is fishing but it is hard work, especially in the Várgolundur sea, and many of the young folk have turned their backs on the water, instead they flock to the big towns like Ingolfsfell or to Lāngāholt which is a mining village about three leagues form here."

"What about the people of Kāldākinn, do you think they would just open up their arms and welcome us, just like that, I know you did Gufi, but would they, no questions asked?"

"No, probably not, but if you explain yourselves to their council like you did to mine, then I think they would welcome you, yes, they are hardy folk and do not suffer fools gladly, but they know the truth in their hearts."

"What is that, the truth in their hearts?"

"Their village is dying, the population is aging and even now they don't have the man power to land the minke whales which was their main source of income and if by chance they do, well they have to call out for help to land and process them, all of which costs money and does not bring in any extra, they are half starved and very desperate."

"Many empty houses and not very many people, you say."

"Yes, and they have a church, but a congregation of less than ten, the priest, well I want to call him a priest is as mad as the rest of them, he calls himself 'brother Cuthbald', I think he is a monk, not a priest because when I call him that he always scolds me, did I mention their church is built from stone, stone indeed, our church is made of wood, do you like wood? I love wood, any you'll see soon enough!"

"So, what is the plan, do we just turn up and offer our help?"

"Good point, instead, I will come with you and I will bring half the wood your people helped bring here, as a sort of thank you and you can turn it over to the village as a good will gesture, then use the wood to build and repair. Do you know that they don't even have any protection from the outside world, no high walls or defence ditches, and look at all of you, so young, strong, and ready to defend the village in a fight, no? And we have all the wood you could possibly need or want, but not for free you understand?"

"Do they need people to fight for them, you said it was far away this Kāldākinn?"

"No, no, I just meant that they couldn't defend themselves from a fart, that is all, nothing more."

"Are you sure this is a good idea, Gufi?"

"Yes, come we must get ready for the journey, I will introduce you formally when we get there, and Rogan, relax, everything will be just fine! They will love all your young people and welcome you with open arms."

The journey to Kāldākinn took until well after the sun was high in the sky, but it stayed bright and warm with a nice fresh breeze and the road was well maintained and made of stone just like the one that lead to Hundsnes, so all were in good spirits. The road snaked around the outer most edge of the forest and a glance over to the right and it there it was a breath-taking vista of rolling hills and valleys, full of every colour of plant you could imagine.

As the long winding procession of horses and wagons entered the arch denoting the beginning of the village, they were slowly met by what looked like every resident left in the village, some walked alongside and many formed a large group to the rear.

There was a continuous amount of small talk from all the residents as they wondered who all these poor unfortunate wretches were, riding with their old friend, Chieftain Grettersson.

The procession came to a halt just in front of the village hall, it was a building similar in size and shape to the one in Hundsnes except where as that was constructed solely from wood this building was constructed with stone, or rather many stones cemented together until about halfway up then with a wooden section the rest of the way to the roof. The roof was made of tiles.

An older man came out to meet Gufi as the column drew to a halt, he carried a staff and his clothes were once quite elegant, alas, now the sands of time had faded their colours and ruffled their edges, but they demonstrated authority all the same.

"Gufi Grettersson! How good it is to see you my old and dearest friend." He whistled through a toothless mouth.

"Renwick Heldur, you, old seadog you, I see you managed to survive another winter, how are things in Kāldākinn?"

"Oh, you know Gufi Grettersson, life has its own rewards, we have our lives and a roof over our heads, but what brings you here, and look at you with so many mouths to feed, are you an army on the march, you look worse than ragamuffins?"

Renwick eyed the newcomers with deep suspicion, but before another word was said between them, Renwick had to shout above the noise of the gathered crowd for quiet, so that the two chiefs could continue with their conversation.

"These poor unfortunate and homeless wretches are friends of mine who have fallen on hard times and who are looking for somewhere to call home, somewhere where their skills are needed and that they can build into a safe and secure home for everyone, look at them, why they could even contribute to the prosperity of your crumbling village, don't you think?"

"What! Have you become a sorcerer since last we met? Stop speaking these words of enchantment! Are my ears playing tricks on me, or are you actually asking me if we can take them in, all of them, have you gone mad in your old age Gufi?"

"Renwick!"

"No, no, no, none of your flannel, the answer is no! and before you utter a single word tell me why are most of the menfolk green, are they pretending to be Orsk, I know a real Orsk when I see one, and why pray tell do they stink worse than old man Porgies fish factory, and that is saying something!"

"Renwick, let me explain, but not out here, let's go inside and show our guests your wonderful hospitality."

"Wonderful hospitality indeed, why, do you not just come out and say it, free food and drink at my expense!"

Rogan asked Ongar to join him, but he turned to the rest of his people and said to camp here in front of the village hall and to make campfires ready cook food. Brenn asked where they should get the food from and Rogan said to send hunting parties out into the fields as far the edge of the forest and catch whatever they could and share the cooked food with the villagers as they really did look half starved, many with sunken cheeks and dark black rings around their eyes.

Inside the once great hall that was now the village hall, four of the council members or elders of Kāldākinn already sat, Renwick made five and the other seven empty chairs were from members who had passed away and not been replaced. Some of those who saw themselves as prominent members of the village did not wait for an invitation and they also crammed inside the hall, they also wanted to hear Rogan's petition and they wanted to have a say on the outcome.

Rogan took nearly three hours re-telling of all of his people's lives prior to arriving at Hundsnes and he spared no detail. When he had finished, he faced a barrage of questions from every quarter, it was impossible for him to answer until Renwick picked up his staff and banged it heavily on the floor three times. Renwick asked the first question, "So, you escaped the Orsk of Obreā, but won't they follow your trail, a trail that leads right here, and won't they want to exact revenge on not only you but on us for harbouring you?"

"No, they won't, the Orsk I believe still hold on to their traditions, so they believe that their gods had blessed our victory, but that the price was too high for some of them to bear, and as I said these were unusual times, a human winning this contest I told you about, the fight between Lōrnicā and themselves, they have their own traditions and codes and they dealt with me as they saw fit, I had not broken any of their codes. The other two warband leaders should have at least told me what they had planned even if it were a bad plan that lead to defeat I would have followed it, that is my honour, my code, but they choose another path which lead to their own downfall, that was on them."

"You talked about a new generation of half-bloods and humans but forgive me if I ask where they will get their women from, might they not just come here to take them, or even follow your tracks to Hundsnes?" asked another councillor.

"If they do, my warband will protect you, but I just don't see why they would recapture women they have already banished as a bad lot," replied Rogan.

"He has a point, Councillor," remarked Renwick.

"Let me see, you want to bring so many hungry mouths to my village, and then give you not just our food but many of our houses as well, and what do we get in return, do you even have coin?"

"We brought you some wood for repairs, but more than that we can help each other, you could teach us all we need to know to help with your fishing industry and with farming crops, we could make arms and armour along with weapons and I think build defences so that any attacker might think twice before attempting anything."

"Nobody has attacked this village in a generation or more. Last year, we sighted a long boat coming up from the south, even that turned back when whoever it was realised that they were attacking an empty village, as for any trade with the outside world, the last time we had traders here from Ingolfsfell was over a year ago, even the Sherriff doesn't bother to collect taxes anymore!"

"Then help us to help you to put Kāldākinn firmly back on the map!"

Suddenly, the doors of the hall were swung open, and a breathless village came inside excitedly beckoning all to come outside immediately.

As they all filed outside and stood on the steps to the village hall and looked out on a sea of newcomers and villagers all intermingling, the sound of laughing and music and even singing became apparent.

"What is going on here!" Demanded Renwick angrily.

"Look, the newcomers have caught rabbit, squirrel, deer and birds and they are sharing it all with our people, this is a great day of Kāldākinn, the one true God has answered all of our prayers!"

Rogan signalled to Brenn and Willem to bring some of the food to the council members, and Aatu who had until now been very quiet himself suddenly burst into an impromptu dance around the two boys' legs yapping and yelping, everybody who saw the small white dog burst into spontaneous applause.

"This is the white Warg whelp you told us about Rogan?" asked Renwick.

"Yes, this is Aatu, the one so named by the Orsk shaman." Rogan knelt as he spoke with such affection for his little bundle of joy and held his hands out for the creature to leap up on his leg and begin to vigorously lick his face.

"Well, my fellow council members, I should really call for a vote, however, it would appear we have been out voted already. Welcome to your new home, Rogan, now let us all eat I for one am famished!"

The celebrations went on long into the night and everybody ate until they could eat no more and drank until they could neither stand nor sit anymore, and it was late the following day before anyone began to stir from their slumber, most of the village slept outside on the green Infront of the village hall.

Rogan and Ongar began to wake their people and tell them to get themselves ready for the day ahead. At one time, the village boasted a population of over five hundred men, women and children now it was nearer half that amount and so many houses lay empty with cold hearths and decaying walls and roofs.

"I think the only fair way to divide these properties up is by order of seniority, so, this is what I want each of you to do, each male, human or half-bloods, you have to choose if you want to live on your own or ask one of the females to share with you. You women, you have the same choice to make, there will be no ill will if somebody is asked but they refuse, the women who have small children must be provided for by the one who picks them or they must determine to go it alone, do you all understand?"

"Yes, Rogan Ragisson." They all shouted in unison before bursting out laughing at his new name and perhaps their newfound luck.

"Good now who is the next most senior warrior after Ongar and myself?"

One of the half-bloods from Chief Lug-Ran's old unit raised his arm sheepishly.

"I have a silver bracelet, Rogan, so it is I!"

"Do you wish to ask a woman to move in with you?"

"Yes, I do." And he walked over to a woman called Brunilda who had one small boy and who looked as though she was pregnant with her second.

Rogan didn't need to ask the women for she squealed with delight and ran into the arms of Gnarga Ingamann.

This continued for most of the morning before everybody was where they wanted to be, but before they went off in search of their new home Rogan told them to meet back here early the following day to make good on his promises to the village, they now called home.

For the women, there were several options open to them for work, shield maidens, farmers, work in the fish factory, seamstresses or nursery work. For the men, the options were more or less the same except they had to train each day as warriors and they had to help teach those from the village who also wanted to fight, shield wall was a new thing for them, a warband usually meant charging like a pack of wild animals, the fastest and fittest first.

Each third and sixth day of the week everyone who was able helped build the new fortifications around the village, some dug out the ditch while others built up the embankment and yet other chopped and shaped the wood for the palisades.

For the first time in years, the villagers were able to take to the seas again and it wasn't long before they had landed their first minke whale, to which the whole village once more turned out to celebrate. On the seventh day of the week, those who wanted to attend the only building in Kāldākinn that was completely made from stone, were welcome to do so, it was the church.

Brother Bryn Cuthbald was not from Råvenniå originally and his accent sounded vaguely familiar to Rogan but why he did not know. After that first meeting together, brother Cuthbald took Rogan to one side to speak privately to him.

Cuthbald was a tall man standing another inch above Rogan. He had good muscle structure for a man of the cloth which made Rogan wonder if he once was a warrior, his hair was turning white but it still held flecks of black and his short bushy beard was just the same, he wore a full-length off-white rode which matched perfectly his long white hair and trimmed beard. Rogan noticed a sadness in his eyes, or was it regret, he didn't know, but he noticed that this man of God wore only a rope belt around his waist and carried no weapons except perhaps for a small bone handled knife tucked into his belt.

"Rogan, I called Brother Cuthbald, and I serve 'the way' which is not like the established church, that is part of the reason why I left the church, our interpretation of the Holy writings is very different, and what they call a priest I simply call a brother."

"And does our sudden appearance here trouble you, brother Cuthbald?"

"I don't know, Rogan, I just can't put my finger on it, no, I am sorry, that did not come out quite how it was meant. What troubles me is that I feel we have met before, and yet I left Mārcādiā almost five years ago, alas, I am old and my mind sometimes plays tricks, but do you know that you have a Mārcādiā accent, it is music to my ears, it has been such a long time?"

"No, I did not know about my accent, and neither do I know where I am from properly, all I know is that I was a foundling and brought up by foster parents and schooled by the church, before I was captured at a young age by the Orsk and taken to live in the kingdom under the mountains."

"Ah well, don't take any notice of me now, I am sure that I am just being a sentimental old so and so, Rogan, tell me instead about this beautiful creature who never leaves your side, how did you find him, he seems like he is a dog and yet I think he is something else entirely, may I pick him up?"

Aatu was not renowned for letting just anyone pick him up, one or two unsuspecting souls have in fact been barked at or had long white teeth bared at them, but Aatu licked the man of God and nuzzled him this way and that, much to the surprise of both men.

"Are you a man of God, Rogan Ragisson?" brother Cuthbald asked.

"I don't know what to believe, I know I was brought up to be God fearing, I even remember my baptism, the water was freezing cold, but after five years as a prisoner to the Orsk, I just don't know, I did prey every day but I never really thought that I got an answer."

"And yet, here you are, but I thank you for your honesty, this world is not at all how the Almighty intended it to be, we should all be living in peace but as you already know the world is in turmoil, people are too busy plotting and scheming and always looking to make themselves better in the eyes of those around them, and sometimes even at their expense, rather than to just read the good book, it has all the answers."

"Well brother, I have a lot of my own work to do before I can even consider doing the Lord's work, so I don't think I will be of much use right now to either you or him."

"Rogan, I am a great believer in God being able to use whomever he wishes to accomplish whatever his heart desires, anyhow if you need me or just want to talk, you know where I am, until then I will bid you good day."

That night, Rogan had the most terrible dream and he woke several times during the night in cold sweats, He saw a figure of a very well-dressed man and his wife, random names would be called out in the emptiness of his mind, and faces would fade in and fade out, sometimes he fought with the man and sometimes he saw himself in the arms of the women, everybody around him was dressed in the finest of clothes then came the day of the attack when he was innocently at play, and then he would wake up in a cold sweat, and Aatu licked his face vigorously and whimpered in sympathy.

6 One Year On

Setunis was the nineth month of the year and a time when the sun would set early in the west and the nights were getting colder and darker. On odd days, it would rain non-stop and on others the sun would shine, and it was actually quite nice. However, Setunis became the new month of celebration, the celebration of thanksgiving, for the inhabitants of Kāldākinn, for many years the village had been in decline and the population was beginning to age.

Then along came Rogan Ragisson, his nickname, though none were brave enough to say it out loud was, the scarecrow king. To some he was a genuine saviour, to others an opportunity to grow rich and fatten their purses, and yet to others he was seen as a troublemaker, but one year on from his appearance and the village of Kāldākinn was well and truly back on the map. The village was growing exponentially, and traders and visitors firmly set a visit to Kāldākinn as the first place on their journey and no longer a place to be shunned, so much in demand were oil, candle wax, carved bone wear, and seal skins.

In the year that he had been there, Rogan had overseen the complete rebuilding of the villages fishing industry, from landing a handful of minke whales the previous year to whale,

112

porpoise, seal, sturgeon, salmon, mullet, crab and even eel from the nearby rivers.

The fish market was now a thriving business. But that was not all, the farming community had gone from a handful of hens to, the three-field system of crop rotation, with spring as well as autumn sowings.

Wheat or rye was planted in one field, and oats, barley, peas, lentils or broad beans were planted in the second field. The third field was left fallow. Then each year the crops were rotated to leave one field fallow. This system also ensured that the same crop was not grown in the same field two years running.

The farmers even came up with new ways to increase the fertility of the land. They had a saying, that the soil would only give back as much as was put into it. Marl (a mixture of clay and carbonate of lime) and seaweed were used as fertilisers.

Farmers knew that the best fertiliser was animal dung. And while that remained expensive to small holders who could not afford the cost of feeding large numbers of animals, Rogan had introduced a system of rote that allowed the peasant farmers to come and muck out his soldiers stables each day whereby they were able to take whatever dug they could carry away with them at the end of it.

Tenant farmers used to have to give about half their crop away as rent and to pay taxes, but Rogan reduced that to only a quarter and so everybody whatever their trade or Lively hood was starting to really benefit, and it showed in the cut of their clothes.

Where it had once only been woollen garments for the most and linen for the few it was now mixtures of leather, linen, wool, silk and fur, even the colours got brighter, were hues of brown were the main stay of fashion, now it was, Purples, reserved for Rogan and his trusted Household guards, browns, greys, blacks, greens, yellow, crimson and scarlet.

Today was the second day of the month of Setunis and preparations being well under way for the first annual festival of Rogan's appearance, although it has to be said at no time did Rogan or any of his people crave this attention or act superior in any way, their presence was always low key, they just wanted a home and to be happy, settled and safe. Unbeknown to Rogan, the village council had already decided to mark this occasion by announcing Rogan as their new chieftain.

Rogan was delighted to welcome all the visitors in person and stood with a few of his most trusted warriors by the village gates, one of the first to appear was his dear friend Chief Gufi Grettersson and his entourage from Hundsnes, Rogan demanded that he and his immediate family come stay at the old chieftain's manor house by the village hall, it had been left vacant since the previous chieftain died, but kept clean and fresh by the ladies of the village who took it in turns even to put fresh flowers and herbs in every day.

Next through the gates were a delegation from Lāngāholt, the village just below and to the west of Hundsnes, Chief Arn Sigewulfsson had become a dear friend and supplier of much of the stone used to repair and build new buildings around Kāldākinn, even the muddy tracks that passed as roads got a makeover and sewers were cut either side of those new roads instead of being a channel down the centre.

Many traders, new and old, also came through in between these vaunted friends, however, a few of the older villagers became decidedly uneasy when they caught sight of one particular guest and his family, the Sheriff of Ingolfsfell, Magnus Steinolf and in particular his son Skuld. Whereas magnus was stately his son was nothing more than a gutter snipe who made his living off other people's suffering.

The sheriff used to come each year to collect taxes for the king and queen of Råvenniå, and out stay his welcome, but this was the first time in a few years he had visited in person, in fact, ever since the village fell below five hundred people required to call its self a village, now it was seen by many as nothing more than a grubby little settlement that occasionally sold fish and oil.

So, in previous years, Magnus felt that it was beneath him and sent his son in his stead, as you might expect tax revenues were very low for those years and Skuld never failed to register his disapproval on these matters.

Two winters back, he said that seeing as though they had not been catching any whales, he saw no need for them to have the processing factory and so he burnt it to the ground with the old caretaker still inside, of course petitions were made in Ingolfsfell with the Magistrate and the sheriff but it seemed that Magnus was always able to get any charges dropped and the trouble go away.

Today Magnus came by horseback draped in all of his finery, like a returning king, some had pointed out. and as Rogan approached him, he waved to one of his man servants to help him dismount and he walked over to receive Rogan's welcome hand by holding out his right hand upturned for

Rogan to kiss. Rogan thought it better to dispense with that strange custom and instead bowed slightly and smiled.

"You must be the ragamuffin scarecrow; I have heard so much about."

"And you, my lord, must be our esteemed sheriff, Lord Magnus Steinolf!"

"Yes, yes, and I see you must have spent all of last year's taxes on throwing this lavish party, tell me it is not just for me, how could you have known that I was coming after all, I thought my visits were always kept secret?"

"To be perfectly honest, your Lordship if I had known we were in the company of such a beautiful young lady as this, I might even have had garlands put up down both sides of the road."

Rogan teased, "Quite so, quite so, now, please, let me introduce my oldest son, Skuld Steinolf..."

"And who is this delightful creature?" inquired Rogan, interrupting the sheriff.

"Erm, oh this is my dear sweet daughter, Æstrid, >cough< who I see you have already invited yourself to greet."

Ignoring Skuld, Rogan went straight over to Æstrid and he demonstrated no problem taking her by the hand, gently, and kissing the back of that, lingeringly, while he drank in the perfume that she wore, which smelled like the first flowers of spring.

Skuld acted as though he was quite bored and that he was taking no notice of the scarecrow, but deep down he was scathing, and already plotting his sweet revenge of this miscreant.

"I trust you have opened up the old manor house for us to stay, Randolf?" inquired the Sheriff.

"Rogan, my name is Rogan, my Lord, and I am afraid I will have to ask you to find space where you can the village is filling up fast!"

"What about the manor, Rogan?" said the Sheriff with a sullen looking face.

"Full of rats, sire!" Rogan replied plainly, not daring to make eye contact.

"Big fat dirty rats!" Ongar added with a grin on his face.

"Oh, that won't do, no, not at all, well we had better make our way forward before the only place left is to sleep in a barn, heaven forbid, good day to you." And the man servant helped him remount his horse by placing a small wooden foot stool by its side. Then off he went with his family, servants and guards in tow.

Æstrid flashed a flirty smile at Rogan as she rode past him, and he dutifully obliged by smiling warmly in return.

Ingrid Hallgerd, the chief of Rogan's bodyguard, suddenly and out of nowhere stamped the bottom part of her spear on his foot! Apart from Rogan, who caught unawares yelped, everyone one else laughed.

Aethelric the Bard, another who had stayed with Rogan and became a trusted friend, began to sing a little love ditty while strumming his lyre, an oval shaped stringed instrument. Rogan was not amused and made an excuse to return to the village hall leaving those who made fun of him to stay and welcome all the others to the village.

As Rogan walked up towards the village hall with Aatu still happily larking around, he noticed that all the horses and carts that the sheriff and his people had appeared on, were now parked up on the village green, and the sheriff's servants were busying themselves unloading some of the things that he had brought with him.

On opening the hall door, Rogan caught the distinct sound of raised voices, and sure enough Renwick, brother Cuthbald, Magnus, Skuld and a stranger, who Rogan missed at the gate were stood around the table arguing.

"Surely, we have not run out of good ale and fine wine, for what else is there to be in disagreement over on the eve of such a celebration?" Rogan spoke in mock apology.

Renwick turned to Rogan and said, incredulously, that the sheriff had asked to see all of the books from each of the traders registered in Kāldākinn, he said that it was to get a truer picture of our wealth in order to set the taxes for the year. And to see if there were any back dated taxes had been overlooked.

"It's outrageous!" Renwick finished.

"Surely not tonight, Lord Sheriff, why concern yourself with these matters so soon after you have arrived, after all this celebration will go on for the rest of the week, and I am sure that all of the traders will be here for the whole thing, so you can chase these things up later, yes?" said Rogan.

In actuality, Rogan had no idea if the sheriff was trying to push his luck and his authority or if in fact, he could demand to see whatever he liked and so he needed to buy some time while he went next door to speak to his old friend Gufi.

While Rogan made an excuse to leave the great hall, Magnus decided that he and all of his entourage would stay for the duration right here in the great hall, and he began to shoo everyone else outside and start yelling at his servants to put curtains up to section areas off for more privacy later.

Gufi was a mine of information on exactly what the sheriff could and could not do, and even offered to go right over there and tell him to his face!

Rogan thanked Gufi and said instead that after the feast this evening, they might both approach the sheriff in a less public place and when he had been fed and watered, Gufi laughed and told Rogan he was a rascal but shrugged his shoulders and said it was he play.

When Rogan finally walked back over to the Great Hall, he was met on the steps by a very crest fallen Renwick, brother Cuthbald and several of the womenfolk. Even Aatu was beginning to pick up on something else not being as it should be.

"What is it now?" Rogan asked nobody in particular.

Renwick and brother Cuthbald began to speak at the same time then they both stopped and said, 'after you', before neither spoke at all.

"Renwick, you are the Alderman here, what is wrong now?"

"Rogan, that thieving bloated self-opinionated worm has only gone and said that his party will stay in the Great Hall!"

"And that is where these dear people" – Rogan turned to the Ladies and servants – "have placed all the food for the celebrations tonight, all right I see, well Renwick, tell me who does the Great Hall belong too?"

"Since the Manor house was constructed for the chieftain to live in the sheriff does have the right to stay in the Great Hall while he is here on official business, but he knows he is just throwing his weight about now, and he is just trying to wind us up."

"Renwick, go to the gate and fetch my warriors back here, while I go in and see just game our dear Sheriff is playing."

Rogan strode up the stone steps and through the closed Great Hall doors, to his shock the sheriff had already invited all of his people to sit and eat and drink from the food that had been placed there. Rogan approached the sheriff with a face like thunder and his son, Skuld and the stranger could see it and both rose from their seats with their hands on their swords.

"What is the meaning of this?" Rogan was at boiling point. The sheriff hadn't even bothered to stop eating or rise from his seat, that was a very specific insult to Rogan's standing.

"You, common peace of filth, how dare you address my father in that way!" spat Skuld while still visibly holding the top of his sword. The stranger just smiled, the sort of smile that a predator would smile while its prey sat only a heartbeat away and totally unaware.

The sheriff had made his point and eventually he stood up and addressed Rogan, "Thank you so much for the feast you have provided, if I knew you were going to go to all this trouble just for me then I must say I am impressed and I think I should like to visit more often."

"You actually think we are celebrating a visit from a tax collector?" Rogan spoke those words with genuine distain, not for the sheriff because he had not yet got the measure of them but because all tax collectors everywhere had a reputation for over charging and then skimming a little bit off the top for themselves.

"Not just a tax collector, surely if you had attended some of our gatherings in Ingolfsfell you would know that my family and I are friends with the queen, we have what you call, royal patronage, if you catch my drift?"

"Oh. Well, pardon me my Lord I had no idea it was like that, perhaps it is because we have a king ruling Råvenniå, and I have dedicated this last year to actually serving him, as well as his queen." It had actually never even occurred to Rogan that there was a king or a queen, he was too busy helping the good people of Kāldākinn to rise above what meagre lives they had, he was more of a spread the wealth than hoard it all for himself type.

"Perhaps, anyway if you leave us now and let us all continue eating this fine food, maybe I can forgive you, your first offence as, well, er, you were brought up in a cave and have no idea how to behave properly, now, go, Roderick, you are dismissed."

Skuld and some of the other members of the sheriff's entourage sniggered as they watched Rogan leave his own Great Hall with his tail between his legs and steam venting from between his ears.

Once outside, Rogan called his trusted warriors over to him and told them all about what had happened, they were rightly incensed by the insults and wanted nothing more than to march into the Hall weapons drawn and to kill every miserable one of them, but Rogan checked their enthusiasm and said that he had a plan.

"Renwick, can you and some of my men round up all of the Barleda ponies and bring them here, enough to replace every horse the sheriff came on except for the one Æstrid came on, and replace like for like, putting all the horse furniture on the ponies. Barleda ponies were indigenous to this area and were very short in build with short legs, the saddles would look quite ridiculous on them. After that, when everyone is asleep in the great hall, sneak in and steal all their clothes except for Æstrid, now Ingrid, I want you and your shield maidens to put on your finest dresses and bring ale continually to the sheriff's guards and make sure there is more than enough to drink inside the hall too, now go, everyone as I wish to enjoy what is left of the evening myself."

"Where shall we take the food for the villagers Rogan, there is still much to fetch out from people's homes and there is a lot of meat still on the roasting spits?" inquired Willem.

"Brother Cuthbald, can we relocate to the church?"

"Yes, of course, by all means, we can fetch some tables and set them up out front, inside the church is only for worship, but outside, well, God be praised but I think this will be a night to remember!" said brother Cuthbald.

Everyone played their parts and the rouse went off perfectly and somehow the ale, wine and food tasted that much better and a good time was had by all.

The following morning, the whole village was awakened by the sound of angry raised voices and the clattering of men turning things over and kicking them around.

The noise was of course coming from the great hall, and the villagers formed up in a semicircle outside on the green. Rogan called to his chosen warriors and six stepped forward, "With me and just be careful to follow my lead, I don't want this getting out of hand, and I don't want anyone getting hurt."

All seven began to climb the stones steps to the main doors when suddenly, they burst open and an indignant sheriff stood, in his sweat stained nightshirt with his arms outstretched and bellowing at the top of his voice, "Where are my clothes?"

All of the villagers could now see right inside the hall as the double doors opened quite wide, everyone except the sheriff's daughter were still in their night attire. The sheriff was red faced and in the foulest of moods when once more he demanded to know where his clothes were, but this time he was greeted with a mass of laughter from the villagers.

What made things worse was that his son and the stranger were stood just behind the sheriff in their night shirts, and they were trying to buckle their belts around their waists, but instead getting stuck in the many folds of their night shirts' material.

"Guards!" Magnus screamed in a high-pitched tone.

"Fetch me the horses, NOW!"

As innocently as he was able, Rogan asked, "What is the matter and why all the shouting?"

At that point, Æstrid appeared from behind her father, fully clothed and looking as immaculate as ever, as she glided across the floor and halted just in front of her father and straight in front of Rogan.

"It would appear that my father and his men have lost their clothes, Lord Rogan."

Ongar jested that some would have preferred it to have been Æstrid, who had lost her cloths, and perhaps all of them while she was at it, that comment brought a flash of anger from Rogan who just glared at him!

Ongar bowed his head and muttered that he was sorry.

Æstrid's words were like sweetened honey on the tip of her tongue and unbeknown to him his cheeks were rosy red like the smacked bottom of a naughty baby.

When he turned to the villagers, who were laughing so much, they actually looked in pain, he wanted them to stop, in case it had begun to take strain on Æstrid.

"Silence, my good friends, this is a terrible thing that has befallen our guests, if anyone has any information as to the were-a-bouts of the sheriff's clothes then please set forward and say now, before he increases the taxes for next year to pay for replacing his loss, and please everyone, this is a most serious matter."

A statement which caused another round of withering laughter. Moments later, around a half dozen sheepish guards appeared still in their night shirts and holding the reins of the ponies with all of the oversized horse furniture on them, and the villagers erupted now, some whooped and others cheered and the morning quickly descended into hysterical chaos.

The sheriff actually tried to sit astride the tiny pony and his feet were planted firmly on the ground either side of the ponie's flanks, rather than ride the mini beast it looked like he would have to walk for it so low to the ground was its body.

By now, even Rogan was struggling to contain himself and had to look firmly in the direction of the sheriff's daughter to try to keep a straight face, her beauty was captivating and right now hugely distracting.

Æstrid, was having a hard time not to laugh herself and as she stepped further forward and whispered 'thank you' into Rogan's ear.

"You are most welcome, my lady." That was all he whispered in return.

"Please except my deepest apologies, my Lord, but I think the God of mischief, Kuteus has been having his own fun in the night, give my men some time and I am sure that they can find where your clothes and horses have been taken."

"Well, you had better make it quick then because I unlike my daughter, do not find this in the least bit humorous, now I hope you have all of the money for your villagers' taxes, the sooner I get them, the sooner I can leave this God forsaken place!"

Gufi Grettersson stepped forward with a bag full of coins. "Here, Lord, I had the good graces to advise my Lord Rogan on the king's taxes, one silver coin for each person over the age of twelve, is that not correct my Lord Sheriff?"

"Hmm, of course, I am neither a fool nor a fixer, Scoppi, take the bag off Chief Grettersson!"

So, the stranger had a name after all, he was called Scoppi. Scoppi was a tall slender man who painted his eyes with thick black liner, that certainly gave him a sinister edge, his hair line was receding leaving him with a high forehead, and on his head, he had a shock of jet-black hair that was left to grow upwards and was probably only ever ran through with greasy hands or cold water, he looked incapable of humour, even if he were to be tired down and have his feet tickled with a feather.

Rogan managed to prize his eyes off Æstrid and walk up the stairs and into the great hall, to personally assess the damage and to be able to apologies in advance to those who he would send in to clean it all away.

Once inside, the hall Rogan saw the full extent of the night before and possibly some of the morning, food was strewn everywhere it had looked as if they had been involved in a food fight, plates and tankards lay everywhere too and many were broken, small throwing axes had been left embedded in walls and wall rugs had been torn apart and hug now in tatters.

Furniture was not spared either but that was probably done this morning, but all the same tables were damaged, and chairs smashed and broken in looked as if a battle had taken place.

Rogan felt the pangs of frustration once more but he bit his tongue and said to himself that the prank that he played had at least given the whole village a moment of light heartedness, but it didn't stop him from making the sheriff wait until well after mid-day had come and gone, to get their stuff back, and after all of the villagers had returned to their homes to eat their own mid-day meal.

No food or drinks were brought for the sheriff and his people, instead they were left to mill around the great hall, waiting, and hopefully stewing in their own arrogance.

However, there was one more thing Rogan thought to do and that was to ask the sheriff's daughter if she would accompany him to church, and so he returned after lunch with a basket of food that his servant had prepared and went to look for Æstrid. Aatu was under Strick instruction to stay home!

In Kāldākinn, there was an unwritten custom that those of the poor members of society would attend worship in the morning before the working day began and later in the afternoon when it was too hot to work, the gentry would make their way to church for the afternoon worship.

Rogan hadn't suddenly found religion, although he considered himself a believer at least, but he wanted another opportunity to spend time with Æstrid, and he knew that by now she would be famished, so he washed himself down as

126

best he could with only a small bucket of cold water and he proceeded to get dressed in his finest attire.

The seamstresses of the village had made for him a rich deep purple linen tunic, with an embroidered picture of the outline of a raven, it was in white and Rogan thought it should have been black, but he took every opportunity to wear over his chainmail shirt, much to the disgust of its makers, for they had wanted him to wear it on his days off so to speak, but he loved it, the cut and the colour and he wanted to wear it every day with pride, and so he did, and there were days when it showed, but today wasn't one of them.

The ladies of the village for a bit of a giggle had wanted the picture to have been of a scarecrow, but the seamstresses would have none of it but they did compromise with the raven, it was their little secret that it was a bird motive and not a rampant beast like some were wearing in the bigger towns and the capital city.

Æstrid always looked her best and so it should not have been that much of a surprise when Rogan turned up unannounced to ask for her to accompany him, her father was impressed with the way Rogan looked and he said that his daughter may go with him, but Skuld looked for all the world that there and then he could have run Rogan through with his sword, but Scoppi had a firm hand on him, whispering that the time would come when they taught this impudent pup a lesson.

Rogan walked arm in arm along the road to the church, as slowly as he could to saviour every minute of the way, and the people for their part bowed their heads or curtsied to pay their respects and on a warm breezy afternoon Rogan was able to forget about life, and they took the food that he had brought and they found a nice spot just before the church gate and they sat and they ate and the talked.

A little while after they had finished the food, Æstrid had said that they should attend at least some of the church service and especially has he looked so handsome in his new attire, Rogan looked furtively around half expecting Aethelric to spring out from behind a wall and burst in to song, but he had hoped that he could show off his clothes in church.

Rogan's face was a picture on entering the church when he saw that all of his trusted men, and women, were wearing similar tabards, just in a lighter shade of purple and without the short sleeves, all heads turned as the church door squawked on its hinges as they let themselves in and there were plenty of smiles all around as the perfect couple now graced the house of God, well there was one person who wasn't smiling, but she had already nearly broken Rogan's foot with the base of her spear.

After the service, the congregation filed out of the church and were thanked repeatedly by brother Cuthbald who had planted himself in the main doorway, when Rogan and Æstrid took their turn to say their goodbye, brother Cuthbald, risking the rath of Ingrid, asked when he would be doing a special service for them, Æstrid immediately replied that her Father might have a word or two to say about that, Rogan just stood there and glowed like an over ripe strawberry.

By the time that Rogan and Æstrid had returned to the great hall, her father and his household were getting in their clothes that had as mysteriously return as they had disappeared in the first place.

Æstrid turned to give Rogan a peck on the cheek and she thanked him for the food and his very charming company and she strolled over to her father and gave him a hug and asked when might it be that they were leaving.

On his way out of the hall, Rogan was met by a delegation of his men and Ingrid, they were all still wearing their uniforms and Rogan did have to admit they looked quite the part, there was Ongar, Aethelric, Gunnar, Ingrid and a frantic Aatu who came bounding across the village green outside the hall.

"It seemed a shame to us all that we were to just go home and change back into our old clothes, so we wondered if you would like to accompany us around the village to do a bit of a meet and greet, and to show off the handiwork of our good seamstresses, what do you say, Rogan?"

"Unless you have other plans of course?" said Ingrid icily.

"No, no, I don't have anything better to do than to walk about like a cockerel strutting my stuff with my dearest friends, come on where to first?"

Aatu had other ideas he demanded a lot of fussing first before he would let Rogan move an inch.

"It looks like someone was jealous, Rogan, so you need to be very careful," stated Gunnar.

"I was so not jealous!" replied Ingrid, just before realising that Gunnar had meant Aatu and not her, but it was a real ice breaker and they all laughed together about the whole thing.

As they chose to walk towards the fish processing factory first, it gave the others plenty of time to tease Rogan, but they were careful not to embrace Ingrid, who they knew had formed an attachment to Rogan. "So asked Ongar what is it between you and the sheriff's daughter Rogan?" That caused a few sharp intakes of breath, but Rogan either didn't see the problem or he genuinely had no plans concerning Æstrid, and

Ingrid watched and listened to every word he now said, like a hawk stalking its prey.

"We are from two different worlds Æstrid, and I, come on I mean she loves the attention it gets her when she is with me, but she has blue blood and I have red, we spent some time together, had a laugh and a joke but it is over now."

"How so is it over?" asked Ingrid directly.

"Like I said we are two completely different people, I don't even believe for one minute she likes me, it's just the number of heads it turns, it is good for her as a lady to be liked, I prefer my ladies to be, less delicate."

"Less delicate!" Ingrid spat those words out.

"Yes, you know, more rough and ready, someone who won't break when I actually touch her."

Ingrid walloped Rogan across his arm, hurting herself more than him in the process, which caused her to yelp before she pulled her arm back very quickly. Rogan smiled and took hold of both her hands, and they looked into each other's eyes and were lost for a moment, the others began to make coughing noises, but then stopped when they realised that this was something special that they had.

"Ingrid, I will never find anyone like you, ever, in fact there is no point me even looking!"

Ingrid felt herself melting into his eyes and her inner voice was screaming, *Kiss me you damned fool!*

However, Rogan unaware of the effect he was having on Ingrid, just suddenly pulled away and continued to talk about the fish factory, stating that it was already smelly, and they still had a way to go to get to it. Ingrid found herself for a fraction of a second stood on her tiptoes, lips puckered with only the empty space that Rogan had vacated facing her. She grunted as she turned around and stomped off ahead of the boys, Aatu whined the whole of the rest of the way there.

To everyone's surprise, the factory was in full swing, as soon as fish were being landed, they were sorted into baskets by type and whisked off inside to be gutted and before being sold to the highest bidder back outside on the sea front. Some fish would have been put to one side to be smoked ready for storage in case the winter was an overly harsh one.

Inside, Rogan chatted to some as they went about their work and they really appreciated him for taking the time, none of them used his visit to take time out, the work was fast and furious and they got paid by the number of fish they processed so time was money, and soon enough Rogan had said a general, well done to everyone and he and his companions were on their way again, this time to some of the outlying farms.

Rogan and Ingrid found themselves walking side by side while enjoying the general conversation about anything and everything, they were like star crossed lovers drawn together by some invisible thread, in fact after half of an hour neither realised that they had been walking arm in arm and enjoying the feeling of being as one.

Today is turning out better and better by the minute Ingrid felt as they continued to walk past the small out crops of rocks dotted by mouse-eared chickweed, and the biennial; lilac coloured Råvenniå primrose with mealy stems and lust green leaves.

Ongar kept making silly faces at the others and Aethelric was attempting to sing them a song but without his Lyre, he found it difficult to compose. Nevertheless, there could be no mistaking Rogan and Ingrid were a couple in everything but name, and there was not a one of them who wasn't made up for both of them, but Rogan still maintained his distance much to Ingrid's frustration.

The first farm they came to was run by a man called Godward who kept the hairy Highland red cattle, and his was one of many farms that belonged to the chieftain, except there wasn't one and so Rogan allowed him to keep all of the profits from the business that he conducted until such a time that a new chief could be appointed.

Godward asked after his lad who had apparently joined the village militia, but the others could see the struggle on Rogan's face as he tried to recall the boy, Gunner stepped in and told the farmer that his lad was the pride of his troop and would make a good leader if he ever decided to give up work on the land and turn to the military for a future, that seemed to delight his father who afterward bid them all good day and went back to his herd.

Next up was a chicken farmer whose range was squashed in between the last farm and the next, chickens it seems did not require the same amount of space as cattle, Athelmund was the name of the farmer and he was as polite and jovial as the last one, except when Aatu had to be held by his collar, it would seem that the he was greatly excited by chickens and wanted to be released so that he could chase them here there and everywhere, which would not have had to same effect on the chickens as it would have on Aatu.

It was in fact at this exact moment that Rogan on attempting to get hold of Aatu before he went for the chickens, that he realised that his right arm was entwined with Ingrid's left, and it took a moment to uncouple them both and look awkwardly away in different directions. Ingrid caught the eyes of all the others, and they smiled encouragingly back at her, but it made her scowl again in frustration.

Next, they headed back towards the main part of the village where they stood and watched as fighters were put through their paces by Halla, Atli, Sigrunn, Brenn and Willem. Halla called over to the group but was looking at Ongar while she did and he acknowledged her with a wave of his hand and a broad smile on his face. It was while they were watching that Solveig had caught their eye, she was like the warband's Apothecary.

Solveig had been trained and skilled in the arts of medicine, dispensing herbs, and medicine that she prepared herself, and she even offered general medical advice and services to others outside the warband, however, some thought her a witch, but that accusation came without any substance, to many she was a blessing, and to the warriors too, as she was able to stich wounds better than anyone Rogan knew, some of the women in the village said that her needle work was that of a lady's handmaiden.

She had a darker side to her, and that could be seen plainly once she had a sword in her hand, in one manoeuvre where she had to swing and slice a bag of hay that was hanging from a wooden post, her swing carried so much ferocity that the side of her blade hit the post, missing the bag, and almost slicing the post in half, Olpaz, her half-blood team mate had to pull the blade free because she couldn't.

They had been paired together from the beginning when warriors were pairing up by rank bracelet, as neither of them had any rank back them, Solveig was dark and moody, Olpaz was just a lost half-blood who latched on to the girl and followed her everywhere like a lapdog, truth be known she hated it and was constantly sharp with him, and he could never do anything right in her eyes.

Halla on the other hand was a little firecracker, adept with any type of bladed weapon, her temperament had a hairy trigger, and it scared most men away, although at first her beauty would have matched that of Æstrid's if she ever kept her self-clean.

However, practice made perfect as she would say and she was never as happy as when she was rolling around in the dirt fighting with someone, unless it was Ongar, who she was committed to, perhaps those two had more fun together than rolling around in the dirt? Many a time was that she got a little worked up and took things too far and it was then that you called Ongar over, and he merely had to look into her eyes and she was like clay in his hands.

A runner came over to the group as they continued to linger by the fighters, he had come with urgent news, the council and more specifically the Alderman had requested Rogan's attendance.

Rogan thinking it was for something serious called one of the mounted combatants over and took his horse. On arriving at the great hall, he slid out of the saddle, tossed the reigns to a servant and climbed the stairs two at a time.

All of the council members were there and already seated and a breathless Rogan wanted to know what the emergence was, it took them no time in telling straight. "We the village elders have been deliberating a serious matter that has arisen in the village this last year, and we have just now taken a vote on this matter…"

"Please, Renwick, cut to the chase, I am a busy man!"

"Who, all right, if you are going to be a sour puss, we have decided on who will be our new chieftain!"

"Okay, but what as that got to do with me, you are the ones in charge, are you not. It is your discission."

"It is indeed, and it is binding, and that is why we have chosen you, Chieftain Ragisson!"

7 Revenge

It happened on the night of the twenty third of Setunis when the sun had set in the western sky some hours before. Nobody knows how or when precisely it happened as the bodies were not found until first light the following morning when the first traders came to the villages main gates which still remained closed.

Rogan and Ongar were called together with his trusted warriors and they found all eight of the gate guards dead, each had been taken down one at a time but not killed straight away, there wounds were consistent with being surprised and incapacitated before the assailant had returned to each of them and mutilated them and left them to die slowly in their own blood.

Each individual had been gelded and had their eyes and tongues cut out, in all of Rogan's seventeen years he had never seen anything like this, even the Orsk wouldn't have used such butchery. Humans can be the worst of all types sometimes, and whoever laid claim to this handy work was already high on Rogan's list of revenge targets.

Rogan thought instantly that this in fact was a revenge killing by the sheriff for the humiliation he had suffered and it sent out a very powerful message to the whole village, you are not as safe as you thought you were, because this did not happen in a matter of minutes or even an hour, this level of violence took hours to complete.

Rogan wanted revenge on the sheriff and was about to order all of his mounted warriors to their horses and ride to Ingolfsfell immediately. However, Ingrid Hallgerd, the newly appointed Captain of his Shield Maiden's stopped him, by saying that he is a chieftain now and he can't just go off half-cocked, first he must gather evidence, and go through the facts by process of elimination.

First the gates had to stay closed and all of the traders and people who wanted to enter or leave the village had to be re-routed to the eastern gate, the one near the fish factory. So, his trusted warriors began to set Rogan's wishes in place, and to make sure that no one got too close to the crime scene.

Rogan, Aethelric, Ingrid and Halla all paced about looking for clues and Ingrid spotted that nothing had been taken, each of the guards still had their weapons sheathed and their shields had fallen almost at their sides as they each fell, Halla said it was a fully trained assassin someone who knew his craft and enjoyed it a bit too much.

"Aethelric thought that if the gates were closed then the assassin must have had inside help or they were able to fly over the high walls. But who in the village had an axe to grind, there were suspects, as people had been overheard to say that they resented having the half-bloods in the village, but they were just the regular villagers, weren't they?"

"Even Solveig had expressed her annoyance to being paired with Olpaz the half-blood, and she can be really cruel to him, I have seen this, but if we start accusing our friends then were will this end?" Rogan interjected.

"Halla said that the removal of the male genitalia was definitely a statement. Is a man really a man if he has no stones, was it a power thing? Did someone feel that humiliated that they had to debase these men?"

"When we go into battle, we have but one wish, one prayer, that if we are to die then let it be with a weapon in our hand, to take that feeling away is to take a man's courage away," stated Aethelric.

"This, rules out the Orsk, in my opinion, nothing that I am seeing is telling me that this is their work."

"Do you still think it is the sheriff, Rogan?"

"More than ever, but Ingrid is right we cannot just ride into Ingolfsfell and accuse him he will have paid men who will swear under oath that he was with them all day, yesterday. He even intimated that he had the queen's ear, if it was perpetrated by him then we will have to plan our next move carefully."

"Are all agreed that this is the work of the sheriff, then?"

"Aye," said everyone present.

"Then our next move is to go to Ingolfsfell and report it, he is the sheriff, and so he will have to investigate, that's the part of why we pay our taxes, and if we can lure him here and we can spring a trap of our own," mused Rogan.

Out of his most trusted warriors, Rogan would select twelve of them to accompany him on this mission, four shield maidens, four men and four Hal-bloods, and Aatu. They were, Solveig, Ingrid, Sigrunn, Halla, Gunnar, Atli, Leowyn, Ceolric, Ongar, Waruk, Olpaz and Malthu.

Rogan told them to pack supplies for just a couple of days, and to prepare themselves for the journey to the Ingolfsfell the following morning, but first things first, these dead guards would need to have a proper burial, and so Rogan and Ongar headed over to the Church to meet with brother Cuthbald. While some of the trusted men who were going carried the bodies behind Rogan and Ongar.

Brother Cuthbald agreed that this was a most hyenas crime the like of which he had never seen, and he was now in his fiftieth winter. "I know this will be hard for you Rogan but you must now let the proper authorities deal with it as they see fit, any interference on your part and they will think you have an axe to grind, you are a chieftain of a village that stands on crown property, and the rightful representative is the sheriff through the Jarl, if as you suspect they the sheriff is involved then be clever and entrap him,"

"It would be easier to have him meet with an accident here while investigating these murders, brother."

What does the good book say, thought Rogan Ragisson, Kristosiān's chapter twelve, verse nineteen. "Do not avenge yourselves, beloved, but yield place to the wrath; for it is written: 'Vengeance is mine; I will repay',", says Ělyāh.

Whilst two men each dug the eight graves Rogan and the brother went over what might be the best course of action when reporting what had happened.

Brother Cuthbald warned from the outset that this might be a trap, either on the journey there or once they were in the town, to lure Rogan out from under the protection of his men.

Ingolfsfell was ten times the size of Kāldākinn, the brother explained, and it had a standing army of over a thousand trained soldiers who were barracked not far from the palace.

Rogan couldn't even imagine the size of the place, but he knew that he soaked up every scrap of information, if he was to have a plan of action, he needed to know as much as he could.

Cuthbald advised that the four half-bloods go dressed as monks and he was very specific as to what they should wear if they were not to be hindered by the gate guards.

"A monk's clothes were designed to cover all of the flesh, first, linen underclothes, hose or socks, and a simple woollen tunic tied at the waist by a leather belt. Over these was their most recognisable item of clothing, the cowl. A monastic cowl was a long sleeveless robe with a deep hood. On top of that cowl another robe was worn, this time with long sleeves, do this properly and they may as well be invisible, get it wrong and they may as well be naked."

"What about the others?"

"Pair them up! They will be traders, Leowyn has a beard and looks older than he is, he should be Solveig's father, she is young with a flat featureless face that always looks sulky, she will be the stroppy teenage daughter, Atli and Sigrunn to inseparable young lovers, Heaven help them, just tell those two to be themselves, but not too much they will be in public, and we don't want them arrested for indecent behaviour!"

What about the other four?

"Let me see, Gunnar is the older brother, Ceolric the younger, Ingrid can be Gunnar's wife and Halla, Ceolric's girlfriend. The monks will be travelling to the main church in the town centre until they pass into the town then they can shadow the rest of you should you meet any trouble."

"Ongar the monk, he will lover that!"

Okay. "Father and daughter are just going for the market, perhaps to buy a new dress, or something. Atli and Sigrunn are just married so they are on a sightseeing trip, the others

140

are the market traders going to the market to sell their wares, hence the wagon packed with goods."

So, the plan was for them to travel together most of the way as a caravan of travellers and traders heading south, then before you approach the road to the main gates of the town split up and mix with all the other people who will be entering the town gates that morning, don't be late and don't be too early, and don't do anything to make the guards suspicious, they are trained and on the lookout!"

Everything was now set, all they needed was to wait for the moon to finish its journey across the night sky, and by now it had already gone over halfway. "Go get some rest, you are going to need a clear head in the morning."

The journey to Ingolfsfell from Kāldākinn was a total of thirty three leagues and by horse it should take around eight and a half hours, but given that they would be travelling with at least one wagon you could add a further three hours, even though the road is pretty straight and was constructed by the Kristosiān's out of hardcore and stones. So, brother Cuthbald had advised that they find somewhere to stop overnight, as it would be silly to arrive for market at midnight.

The morning was bitterly cold and those who had nothing to do stood and patted their hands on their sides while exhaling curls of vapor, once the wagon was packed and checked for any sign of the concealed weapons, it was time to set off.

The first part of the journey was again the breath-taking sight of the rolling hills and valleys, the splashes of colour that interceded the banks of fog and mist that rolled downwards and away from the road, it was hard to see how this plan would pan out, or even if any of the twelve would ever see these beautiful views again.

Rogan's mood was sombre the further away from the safety of Kāldākinn, even Aatu running around and leaping and sticking his nose into every bit of hedge way and his constantly trying to leap up on Rogan's lap was doing nothing to lighten his master's mood.

The chieftain, even wondered if they should turn right at the fork in the road and visit his friend Gufi in Hundsnes and maybe even pick up some more men to accompany them, but a journey like that would add another thirty leagues on to their travelling and that was without adding all that it would take to get back even this far, and time was of the essence.

Leave this matter too long and the fire goes out in one's belly, the feelings of revenge that smoulder like a well-fed fire eventually grow cold and are forgotten, and those men deserved better, and they will have their justice, one way or another.

Rogan felt like he was carrying the weight of the world on his seventeen-year-old shoulders, but he had been given the title of chieftain and with that came responsibility and so, he had no choice, he had to be strong, and positive, and that meant standing on his own two feet, Kāldākinn expected it, his trusted warriors expected it, and his own moral compass demanded that he set a good example.

So, at the crossroads, he pulled the reins of his horse to the left, deciding against a visit to Gufi, a visit to Ingolfsfell it would be and so instead he busied himself making a fuss of Aatu who had finally jumped up on to the saddle of his horse and was trying to position himself so that he didn't slip right back off.

As they turned into the junction, Rogan did glance longingly to the right, towards Hundsnes However, Ingrid, who was now alongside him pulled gently on her reins to the left, and if Rogan hadn't of stayed left himself then their horses would have collided, the die was being cast, now all he needed to do was to have the courage to do the right thing.

After about six hours on the road, Rogan called for a break. He wanted them to pace themselves, and so they pulled the wagon off the road and set about making a small camp fire to cook some of their rations on, Waruk and Malthu offered to go hunting for small animals, and Rogan said, Yeah, that would be good, but be careful you are supposed to be monks!

"Monks have appetites as well you know, Rogan!"

"That's as may be, but don't make it look like you are skilled with weapons that's all I am saying."

The two half-bloods climbed over a low dry-stone wall that ran the length of the road on both sides except for the parts here and there that had been damaged or just robbed away, once they were on the other side they were immediately taken back by tens of thousands of wildflowers in bloom, that were attracting many rare insects and birds.

The higher up the slopes they went, the trees got shorter and shorter, until they could no longer grow. Here the landscape is open and subjected to high winds, but it made it easy to sneak up down wind of rock ptarmigan's and Boreas hares, and either of them would make a tasty supper. They had been away from camp about an hour when they returned with six of the plump birds and a brace of hares.

After the food had been consumed and the evening was fast becoming night, Rogan gave instructions for who would take first watch and then who would replace them every two hours until daybreak. Ingrid took this opportunity to unroll her fur blankets next to where Rogan had placed his, however Aatu had other ideas and he took the centre ground leaving Ingrid very frustrated once more. "Stupid mut!" she whispered in Aatu's ear as she lay down at the side of him. Aatu turned his head towards her and began to vigorously lick her face. "No, Aatu, we are no longer friends, you and I!"

The following morning just as the sun rose in the eastern sky, the group readied themselves once more for the road, muscles ached and each in turn yawned as they were no longer used to sleeping in the open air on hard ground, Ongar remarked that they were getting old to which his women, Halla Greilanda said that perhaps she should start looking for a younger fitter warrior for husband material, to which they all laughed, some smacking Ongar on the arm and telling him he was either already married or very much under the thumb, which both amounted to the same thing really.

At sixteen years of age, Halla was an intoxicatingly beautiful woman with long blond hair, where it was not matted with mud, down past her shoulders, and a figure that belied her strength but demonstrated her agility especially in combat, but what Halla had gained in looks she had definitely lost in temperament, she was a wildcat easy to provoke and hard to calm. Ongar loved her dearly as he too was a true warrior at heart and even though they were these days inseparable they had no plans to marry or settle down and have children. Every one of their days was lived as though it was their last, they were truly the last of the berserkers.

After another five hours on the road Rogan decided that they would stop for one last time before and he found another secluded spot, he thought, for them to make camp and spend a second night under the stars. This time, Rogan thought it better if the monks didn't go hunting as they were too near to Ingolfsfell now and that in fact they should make a second camp a few paces away from the others, as monks would not ordinarily mix with ordinary folk.

Atli and Sigrunn were asked to hunt for supper this time, and once more Rogan clucked over them like a mother hen, be careful, be quite and stay safe, they both said in unison, "Yes, Mother!" Before disappearing into the early evening.

They had been gone something near two hours when Rogan began to pace back and forth and Aatu copied his every move, Halla said for him to stop and that he would wear a hole in the ground if he didn't, and anyway they were probably cosied up together somewhere nice and warm and had forgotten the time. Rogan stopped and was about to send Ingrid out to look for them with Gunnar when they both reappeared, Ongar said, "I think we are going to need a bigger fire!"

Atli, wearing this biggest grin on his face had slung around his neck a large red deer with enough meat to feed them for days, everyone cheered and Halla and Ingrid started to make the fire pit bigger, while Leowyn looked around for branches that could be turned into a spit. "So, who would like the job of skinning this beast?" asked Atli.

The four half-blood monks said that they didn't mind doing that job. "If you remember it was always Olpaz and Waruk that did it when we were back at the cave village. The very mention of their time there made Solveig shiver, Rogan reminisce on just how far they had come in a little over a year, and each of the others each momentarily lose themselves in memories, both good and bad."

Once the animal was skinned and its innards gutted, it was prepared for the ad hoc spit, Aatu greedily chowed down of the parts that were discarded. After the deer meat was cooked, they ate their fill of it and there was still over half of the beast left, Rogan was worried that the smell it could attract unwanted guests in the night and told Ceolric and Olpaz to dig a pit and bury what was left to cover its smell.

Ingrid suggested that it be wrapped in linen cloth first so that it could dug up in the morning so that they could all have a hearty breakfast, she said it was just such a shame to let it go to waste. Rogan shrugged his shoulders and said it sounded like a good idea, and so that is precisely what they did.

The second night was not as peaceful as the first, at some point in the night one of those on guard duty, Olpaz, one of the half-bloods, heard rustling in the bushes about sixty away paces from the camp. If he had thought it to have been an animal, he might have just ignored it, but something in his gut told him otherwise, and he cupped his hands to his face and began to make a sound like one of the wild animals of the night and within seconds everyone was awake, eye open not moving a muscle but weapon in hand and ready to defend themselves.

Aatu, who incidentally had allowed Ingrid to cosy up to Rogan this time, was up like lightening and he did not wait, instead he homed in on the noise and ran straight as an arrow towards the sound, and within seconds the howling voice of a human was heard as the white warg seized whoever was lurking there by the ankle, and dragging him or her to the ground.

"Get your damn dog off me! I was about to introduce myself when it attacked me, god darn it."

146

"Walk into the light so that we can see who it is and then I will call him off," replied Rogan.

"I am Tostig Seaward, and I am with two other companions, Harek Kormak and Sighadd Ketilbiorn. We are journeying to Ingolfsfell and we saw your fire from a distance and hoped to join your group, look none of us have drawn weapons, please believe me."

"Aatu, heel! Tell me, Tostig, where are you from and why do you journey this far, just the tree of you and without any provisions?" inquired Rogan.

Looking at the most unlikely three people you would ever think to see together, Rogan began to scrutinise them a little more while they spoke. Tostig was a young man of his own age, but already his hairline was receding, his hair was dark brown as were his eyes, he had a remarkable stern look on his face like he thought he was better than anyone else, and actually speaking to Rogan, and his ruffians was painful.

Rogan also noticed his well-manicured hands and his soft complexion, this boy had lived a pampered life and he was no fortune seeker, he looked to all the world like spoiled rich brat, and his squealing earlier did nothing to dissuade Rogan, the other two were his hired thugs.

Harek might as well of crawled on all fours he was so dirty and smelly, his hair was shaved off both sides of his head and he kept a thick mop on top of brownish black hair which also hung lankly over his left eye, on his right-side scalp he bore tattoos of a once proud warrior, who now wore rags and skins to keep himself warm, unlike his compatriot.

Sighadd was a bearded slightly older former warrior who had also fallen on hard times, that was borne out by the present company he kept, his hair was a lighter shade of brown and was just left to hang where it grew, his clothes however said that he retained some self-respect, he wore a tidy leather jerkin and woollen tunic and trousers.

"We are from a small farmstead out west, called Ghentweald, and we go to seek our fortune, life is to boring where we are from, surely you understand, no?" said Tostig with a half-smile.

"What makes you say that Tostig we do not know you, and you do not know us, our lives are hard and we try to make an honest living, we are but humble traders who have banded together with those monks to keep safe, like that of which you now seek."

"I beg your pardon; I mistook you for warriors but in my defence, you do not have the way of a trader about you and I am certain that if I were to haggle for your goods, I would see your build and fearsome demeanour and simply agree to whatever prices you wished to sell at."

"Ah, but look I am mistaken, and we have all explained ourselves and can now be friends surely, and may I inquire if any of that meat I saw you dig up is going spare we are starving," said the silvery tongued Tostig. However, he was soon left looking bemused as the traders started to put on what looked decidedly like chainmail armour and leather jerkins and the each in turn checked the edges of their swords for sharpness.

"I'm guessing Ingolfsfell is a hard market to sell at if traders have to dress this way that is."

After a hearty breakfast that was shared by all, it was time to roll up the sheepskin bedding and pack away the cooking equipment and when everything was stowed away Rogan said it was time to set off as they were hoping to arrive early to get a good place at the market, the sun was rising just ahead of them as the road snaked east wards, and they were joined in their caravan by the three newcomers.

The company was ambling along at the speed of the horse drawn wagon when out of nowhere a single arrow fizzed through the air and hit Ceolric Brocwulf who was driving the wagon, in the chest just to the left of centre, killing him instantly, and causing his body to slump forward and fall between the horses and out of sight.

"Ambush!" yelled Rogan as everyone dismounted and dove for cover. A few more arrows fizzed by and overhead, this time one found its mark in the horse on the left side of the wagon, wounding it grievously.

"They are both sides of the road," Ongar called out.

"How many?" asked Tostig.

"I can't see anything with the sun in my eyes!" shouted Gunnar Helgisson.

Rogan cursed his luck as he had once before been caught with the sun in his eyes, he spat on the ground and said a little something by way of a prayer to whomever might be listening.

Aatu, was not now nor ever been one for a thoughtful strategy, and doing what any came naturally on impulse, he broke into a charge and veered to the right side of the road where there was a low stone wall.

Ingrid, and her shield maidens, Halla, Sigrunn and Solveig kept their bodies low and shields high, and ran after the white warg. Now all the arrows were concentrated on the warg but he was too fast and to willey and they all missed him and pinged harmlessly off the dry-stone wall.

Atli and Leowyn saw their chance to attack, and they hopped over the low wall near the wagon and followed in the direction of the shield maidens.

"What should we do?" asked Tostig, but before he could get a reply the four monks, Rogan and Gunnar were angling Left and bolting forwards themselves. Tostig and his two companions opted to stay by the wagon in case anyone should try to run off with it or its valuable cargo.

Whoever the hidden assailants were, they were soon overwhelmed in combat and began to fall one after the other until just two were left alive, one either side of the road. Rogan shouted for them to be spared, he wanted information and to get that, these two at least, had to be kept alive, the rest who had died were soon stripped of anything valuable or useful and their bodies disposed of behind the low stone wall.

The two captives were tied to the two left side wheels on the wagon while four of Rogan's warriors uncoupled the horses to take of the one that had got injured. Two of the others took Ceolric Brocwulf's lifeless body and began to dig a shallow grave for him which they would eventually cover with stones from a section of the wall so that wild animals might not be able to get at his body.

Ongar took up questioning the first prisoner, "Who are you and why did you attack us?"

The prisoner looked at Ongar and spat on his boots.

Rogan hit the second prisoner across the face with the wooden end of his axe causing his mouth to bleed proficiently.

Ongar asked the same question again, and the prisoner still refused to speak.

Rogan raised his hand to hit the second prisoner again when the man shouted out to stop.

"Why should I not hit you, your friend is refusing to speak?" said Rogan.

"He is not my friend; I don't even know him!" the prisoner hissed between dribbles of blood.

Ongar asked the question again and the first prisoner laughed.

Rogan backhanded the second prisoner again this time hard enough to dislodge a tooth, and the man screamed in agony. "Stop! Please, stop!"

"I will stop when you start telling me the truth!" Rogan spoke his words slowly and deliberately, and the man said, "All right, all right, I will tell you what you want to know!"

Ongar then took a couple of steps towards the second prisoner and asked the original question, but before the other could answer the first man shouted for him to keep his mouth shut.

Rogan whistled just once and Aatu jumped at the first prisoner and bit him right between the legs, and the man screamed and screamed for the creature to be called off, while blood ran both sides of his trousers along with the contents of his bladder.

The second man began to speak so fast now that nobody could understand a word he was saying and Rogan lifted his right leg and stood on the man's groin. "Stop talking so fast or I will introduce you to my pet, you know the one with his teeth embedded in your friend's crotch."

"I'm sorry, I'm sorry, my name is Arnvid and he is Guthorm and we were waiting for a caravan to come down this way ladened with goods to rob. That is the truth, my Lord, I swear!"

Tostig jostled his way forward and told Rogan to look at both their money pouches, up until now the thought had not even crossed his mind. However, when Rogan pulled the pouch from Arnvid he found that it contained many gold coins, Ongar did the same with Guthorm and just the same it was full of gold coins.

Arnvid was a plump man, another former warrior who had got used to rich living, he still had old faded tattoos on his left cheek, his hair was a mass of brown and he had an unkempt beard, his skin was filthy as were his clothes but some of that, but not all, could have been put down to the fight and him being wrestled to the ground before being tied up.

Guthorm was almost as thin and needle like as Arnvid was fat, he had long dark brown hair that hung low beneath his shoulders and it was very greasy, however, his beard was in somewhat better care for it had been cut and shaped, Guthorm wore thick black eye liner, which reminded Rogan of Scoppi, the sheriff's man. His cloths had also seen better days like Arnvid, but he had the addition of a fur cowl around his neck.

Rogan knew that these two worms would sooner die than cross the hand that paid them so handsomely, but in just that fact he had learned so much, this had to be the work of the sheriff and to prove it he would need these two 'would be' bandits alive. "Bind them both and throw them over a horse each, collect their other horses and hitch one to the wagon and put the injured Horse out of its misery."

Rogan then counted out twelve of the gold coins from one pouch and gave one each to his warriors and kept the extra one back to give to whoever should claim Ceolric's body back in Kāldākinn. Then with the remainder in the bag, he threw it to Tostig. "Here have this for your troubles." The other bag that was bulging at the seams he gave to Ongar. "Here keep this for our future expenses."

The party forewent stopping again and instead took dried food from their haversacks to eat, it was getting to be midday and the gate guards would be highly suspicious as it was, with them turning up so late.

As they drew near to the gates, surprisingly there was still a considerable amount of people entering and leaving the town, Rogan hung back until first Arnvid's horse had drawn alongside him and then Guthorm's and he coshed both of them so that their bodies would fall limp once more and they would be unconscious for a time.

The four monks went ahead of the others, Halla, Gunnar and Ingrid now all squashed themselves on the wagon's wooden bench and the spare horses were tied off at the back of the wagon.

Leowyn and Solveig went next as father and daughter, and Atli and Sigrunn followed a short while afterwards, Rogan took a haversack from the back of the wagon and slung it over his right shoulder and proceeded to amble slowly behind the wagon holding the two sets of reigns from the horses which the two prisoners were now laying lifelessly over.

Tostig and his two companions were left behind without so much as a goodbye or see you later, and so they clicked their heels into the flanks of their horses and rode off into the town as fast as they could.

Rogan did wonder if they would give his party away to the gate guards, but he hoped that the gold coins which he passed to them was more than enough to buy their silence, if they ever did meet again then Rogan firmly believed that it would be as enemies.

8 Ingolfsfell

The main gates to the town of Ingolfsfell were most impressive indeed! They were wide enough to allow two rows of traffic to flow at the same time, one going in and one coming out, and there was enough space for plenty of guards to mill around in case there were any problems, just how good those guards were, Rogan didn't want to find out.

The structure itself was whitewashed stone blocks, that had been cut with such procession, they formed a pattern up and down that matched perfectly, and they aligned with the rest of the towns stone wall exactly. The outer arch, as there was also an inner arch, was decoratively made with slightly bigger cut stones, that had been placed around the arch to add to its slender, of which there were seven, one on the very apex of the arch and then three either side, each spaced out perfectly to match the opposite side.

Inside the square tower that formed the gateway, there was two sets of solid oak doors emblazoned with iron work and hinges, they must have stood around twelve feet tall and at least three foot thick, comprising of layers of timber alternating between vertical and horizontal planks. In the space above and in the middle of the tower were a series of smaller holes that could have been for defenders to fire arrows through if the outer gates were ever breached.

Just as brother Cuthbald had said would happen the guards waved the 'monks' through without even a second glance, in fact everyone got through the wagon included except for Rogan, and the horses that he was pulling, they drew the attention of the guards like wasps on a hot summer's day.

First their long spears clashed together to prevent Rogan's passage, then they halted the flow of people leaving and once the area was cleared of people they descended, "Where do you think you're going with two dead bodies on those horses?" one of the guards asked.

Rogan dutifully replied as though what he was doing was a perfectly natural thing to do and certainly nothing to cause alarm, "I am late for selling my goods at market on account of being jumped by a gang of villains as I broke camp this morning!"

"Hmm, if you are a trader where are all of your goods unless you were just trying to sell your horse, eh, answer me that, if you will?"

"Do these two scoundrels constitute a gang officer?"

"Of course not, don't be so impertinent!"

"Exactly, the gang stole all of my wares, these two idiots got greedy and tried to steal my purse, thinking I was unable to defend myself, now good sir, do I look like a fair maiden who is need of any help?"

"Erm, I'm going to say no, on account of your...bone structure?"

"Spot on, my friend, I can see why they put you on guard duty, nothing gets past your attention, anyway, suffice to say I kicked their arses, and here they are!"

"Why did you bring them with you, why not just kill them and leave them at the side of the road?" asked one of the guards.

"Surely not my good man, wouldn't we then be denying the good people of Ingolfsfell a public execution?" Rogan implored.

"Who doesn't love a good public execution Cuthwig?" said a second guard.

"I suppose you have a point, but if you want to find the market and then go to the sheriff's house you will have to take the long way round, his house is near the Jarls castle right over in the south west corner of the town, oh look it would be easier just to show you, Renton, you can take the man!"

Renton began walking up Lower Broad Street, and Rogan followed on horseback with the two prisoners, and Aatu, in tow. After a short while, Lower Broad Street became just Broad Street, and at the end of that street was the large stone-built church of Saint Lawrence, which apart from the castle, was by far the grandest building in the town.

At the church was on the right of a crossroads and this is where the 'monks' should have been dropped off, however they wanted to stay close to Rogan and so they hung back long enough for him to over taken them, Renton turned left here in to the High Street and that was the beginning of the market as well, Leowyn and Solveig dropped off here and now their role would be to keep close watch on the guards and their movements in case things went south and they needed an escape route.

As Renton continued down the High Street passed all of the market stalls, it could be seen that this was a large open space that was bordered by the High Street and Castle Street which then merged into Dinham Street, and it was on the corner of the High Street and Dinham Street that the sheriff's house was situated, and Renton said his goodbyes and returned the way he had come. The Castle was now visible from the corner house as it sat on top of a large sloping hill on the other side of Dinham Street.

As Rogan dismounted and tied his horse to the post outside the sheriff's house, he could see a large barn like building with a set of stocks outside of it, at the far side which could have been a lock up as it had iron bars across the front where the wooden doors would have been.

Next, he brought the other two horses around to the post and tied them up as well. Arnvid and Guthorm were still unconscious, and Rogan had a passing thought that he might have hit them a bit too hard, but he couldn't change that now, and so he left them tied up and across their horses' backs.

"Aatu, stay, watch those two and howl if they come around or anyone tries to untie them, have you got that, boy?"

Aatu understood and in recognition he yapped just once. On entering the sheriff's house. Rogan was met by a youth calling himself Sigegar Youngblood, a young man perhaps around the same age as Rogan, with a mullet of brown hair and with sides that were shaved just above the ear, his clothes were not unclean neither was he, but their cut was shoddy and cheap.

Rogan introduced himself, but only said that he had found these two men unconscious, he didn't mention any of the circumstances of our they came to be the way they were.

Sigegar said that they sheriff wasn't here yet, but that he was 'authorised' to at least come and look and put them in the lock-up if need be.

Gunnar, Halla and Ingrid parked the wagon up at the end of the High Street as near to the sheriff's house as they could, and once they were happy that nobody was taking any notice of them, they began taking out the rolls of linen cloth that hid their weapons from view.

Over on the other side of the street, the 'monks' began blessing people who passed by on their side, they were off script, but it didn't seem to draw attention to them other than the odd passersby who began flicking coins at them and thanking them for the blessings they had just received.

Atli and Sigrunn hung around outside of the lock-up pretending to look across the road and up at the castle.

Sigegar followed Rogan outside and quite unexpectedly blurted out, "What have they been up to now?"

"You know these two, er, drunks, yes?" Rogan improvised.

"Yes of course I do they are two of Skuld's er…acquaintances."

"Skuld Steinolf?" Rogan asked surprised by the frankness of the young man.

"Yes. That's right, do you know him, he will be so grateful that you kept these two out of harm's way, I am sure he will have a little something for you, if you know what I mean?"

"Oh yes, it is no problem, Skuld and I met a few weeks ago in fact. I agree he will be delighted that I brought his two friends here instead of leaving them by the roadside."

"I am afraid I don't understand, you found them by the roadside, have they been robbed and beaten, they do look like they have,"

"Yes, sadly they have!" said Rogan at lease that part of his story was truthful.

"Oh dear, and they were only last night bragging about a big score, perhaps they shot their mouths off to the wrong crowd, eh, the Blue Boar can be a bit rough especially if the regulars think you have a bit of coin?"

"Most definitely, you are very wise my friend, very wise, now anyway can I leave them here and can you tell me when I might be able to see the sheriff?"

"Yes, of course we can put them in the lock-up until they wake up, they may not be in the best of moods, and I wouldn't want them smashing the place up, oh, and I think the sheriff will be back this afternoon."

As Rogan left the sheriff's house, he left the horses tied up and said to Aatu, "Come on boy let us go and look around the market until the sheriff returns." The others who were nearby would have been able to hear what he said, the 'monks' enjoying the coin they were collecting decided to stay where they were, and Atli and Sigrunn followed Rogan at a short distance.

Solveig found a stall that was selling pigeon's, most of which were dead and hung up on hooks above the stall or thy were arrayed along the front counter, Leowyn had no interest in pigeon's and so he left Solveig there while he looked at other stalls.

"Good day to you, trader," Solveig said.

"Good day to you too, are you looking for anything in particular today?"

"Yes, my Columba Livia has a broken wing!"

"Ah, how sad, perhaps I can offer you a replacement, let me see, just one moment, if you please." And the pigeon seller picked up a basket of live pigeon's from beneath his stall and selected one from inside.

"This is a fine bird, a trusty bird that will never get lost on its way home, if you catch my drift."

"I will take it, and does the little leather pouch on its leg come with it?"

"For you, dear lady, I will make an exception, please one copper piece, do you have a carrier?"

"No, I do not, do you have one I could buy?"

"Most certainly I do, for another two copper coins."

Later that day, Rogan and Aatu returned to the sheriff's house and saw that Magnus, Skuld and Scoppi were all inside.

"Rogan! It is so good to see you again, did you ever catch the rascals who took our belongings and horses?" inquired Magnus.

"No, we did not, but I did catch two roughens, are they still in your lock-up?"

"No, I don't believe they are, why, what did they do, nothing bad I hope?"

"Never mind, Sheriff, I have come to report a crime that was committed at my village a few days ago."

"Oh! All right then, you had better tell me so that I can see how best we can help you."

Rogan felt his angry boil up inside, but he knew that he had to keep his cool or this could end very badly for him and all of his warriors. Aatu sensed his masters state of mind and began rubbing himself against his lower legs, Rogan bent down to pet Aatu before he took up telling in detail what had happened to the eight guards at Kāldākinn.

Skuld sat impassively throughout Rogan's account with nothing but a half smile on his face.

"I am sorry to hear this terrible news Rogan, I really am, a trick or jest is one thing, but murder is another thing all together, do you think this is a raid by another group, like the Orsk from whom you escaped?"

"No, I don't think this was a raid, nothing was taken, not even the guards' weapons, this looked more like someone trying to send me a message."

"That is as it maybe but I wonder what is the best course of action, should I return to investigate or would we be better served sending a detachment of soldiers back with, they could always stay a while in your village, perhaps this is a matter for the Jarl to sort out?"

"The Jarl?" asked Rogan.

"Jarl Sigfusson, he is…well the Jarl of Ingolfsfell and so your village is his village, your people his people, and it is for these reasons that we pay our taxes!"

The day was getting quite warm and humid, and Rogan was beginning to wish he no longer had his armour on, it was itchy and uncomfortable, and he wanted to find somewhere to change out of his warrior garb and into something cooler and lighter.

The sheriff must have read Rogan's mind or just noticed that he was fidgety because he suggested that they stop of at the Castle Lodge Alehouse for some refreshments, it was just around the corner and on the way to the Jarl's Castle.

The sheriff and his son along with Scoppi accompanied Rogan and Aatu inside where they ordered a jug of the house's finest ale. Afterwards, they made their way across Dinham Street and up into the castle, each set of guards on duty simply waved the sheriff and his party through.

Before Rogan and Aatu were allowed into the main hall at the palace, he was asked to leave his weapons outside in the care of a young lady with a generous smile and helpful disposition, who only scowled when Skuld met with her gaze.

Jarl Gudrod Sigfusson was a slight man just above five-six in height and he was deep in conversation with two ladies who for the moment had their backs turned on Rogan and Aatu.

The Jarl suddenly distracted by the appearance of the new group peered from around one of the women. "Ah, look who is here, dear ladies, if it isn't the sheriff himself, come Magnus we were just talking about you!"

The two ladies turned to face the newcomers. "Husband! There you are we were just discussing dinner tonight and we were telling Gudrod that he simply must attend and with his handsome son and wife of course."

Æstrid glanced towards Rogan and her face lit up and she nodded a greeting without speaking a word.

"Matilda! Æstrid! What a delightful surprise," remarked Magnus, while wondering if they had secretly moved to the palace as they were here so often.

The Jarl leaped to his feet clapping his hands together with glee. "Oh, I do love a family reunion, don't you all?" His grace's smile was infectious until his eye's set on Aatu.

"Oh, there is a dog! Why is there a dog? I do hope it isn't messy, I have just had these floors waxed!"

Matilda shot a disapproving glance towards her smiling daughter. "Thank you, my Lord, but it seems my husband is here on official business, so I think we had better leave you to it, but don't forget, tonight and bring your son!"

With that, the two ladies shuffled off out of the large room but not before Rogan once again caught the whiff of spring from the scent that Æstrid was wearing, she smiled once more but this time only to herself, she loved the attention of the rough and ready muscle-bound warrior, and she loved even more the effect it was having on her dear brother whom she loathed with a passion.

If Rogan was any judge of character one short glimpse at Matilda Steinolf, he thought, would take the shine off newly polished silver, she was built like a pack horse and had the demeanour of a pit viper, the very thought sent a shiver down his spine.

Magnus tried to placate having Aatu present by saying that the dog was house trained, before continuing to re-tell the entire story that Rogan had related to him, before he turned to Rogan and formally him to the Jarl.

Jarl Sigfusson was simply delighted to finally meet Rogan, he said so more than once, while seeming to hold on to Rogan's outstretched hand for far longer than he needed to.

"So, you are the man who is responsible for making Kāldākinn a jewel in the north, welcome to Ingolfsfell, Chieftain Ragisson and erm, your dog! A real-life Barbarian from the northern frontier!"

Rogan and Aatu stared at each other for just a moment and Rogan were about to address the remark, but then thought better of it and said nothing.

"Forgive me for just one moment while I call all of my courtesans in, they simply must see you, you're so dashing if not a little well ordinary looking."

For the next five minutes or so, all of the Jarls friends and some of his enemies, without his knowledge filed into and then out of the great hall. "Splendid!" the Jarl quipped. Before he was reminded about the white furry thing with teeth and claws, although it was more what could potentially come from its rear quarters that really bothered him.

The Jarl thought it just better to ignore the animal and so there was no more mention of Aatu, just a sharp exhaling of breath, every now and again as it caught his eye.

"The news you bring is indeed very troubling is it not Magnus, and I wonder if like you said this is a job for the army rather than you the Sheriff, what do you think about it?"

"I suggested to Rogan that we might send a small detachment of soldiers back with him for a while, they would be useless investigating the murders, but they might make the people feel a little safer!"

"Why not garrison, the village after all it is incredibly important to us here both strategically and financially, what do say, Rogan? Would you like to pay for a detachment of soldiers, eh?"

"My lord, I did not come here to ask for help, I have warriors enough to deal with any problems like that which might arise, and I am sure you have had quite enough coin from my village for this year, your grace, and anyway I came here to seek justice for those who are responsible for the deaths of my men."

"Quite so, quite so, and it is technically my village, but I see your point, so you believe that your men were indeed murdered and that it wasn't your old acquaintances come back to haunt you, because I am told that nothing was taken, is that correct?"

"The only thing taken were the lives of eight of my warriors, and for what reason?"

"What reason indeed, may I ask, Rogan, have you had any run ins with anyone lately, somebody you have crossed perhaps, or a Ménage à trois?"

Rogan locked eyes with Magnus.

"No, my Lord not that I would imagine would result in so callous an act, so I ask again, if it pleases your lordship, I will ask for the sheriff to return with me so that he and his men might investigate this matter further."

"Sherriff, what do think, return with Rogan see what you can see and then report back here in say a week?"

Sheriff Magnus Steinolf was a shrewd man and he could sense that Rogan had marked him as the one responsible for the deaths of his men, and he saw how the chieftain was trying to arrange the situation so that he would go back to the village with Rogan and his men and that might be the last thing he ever did.

"I am afraid I must decline, Jarl; I have important business here as you may recall, however I do know just the man to send back in my stead."

"Ah! You have someone in mind to return in your stead, is that satisfactory for you, Rogan?"

"I would have preferred to offer my hospitality to the Sherriff but if he is too busy then I understand."

"Excellent, now I to have some pressing business so if you don't mind, I will beg your leave and let you discuss the details as you go, good day to you all, and Magnus I will see you later for dinner."

"With your son, my Lord."

"Yes, yes, with my son, and tell your good lady to stop fretting!"

As the party left the throne room, Rogan glanced over to his left to catch a glimpse of who was next in line to speak to the Jarl, and to his great surprise it was the young man he had met on the road here, Tostig Seaward.

Tostig had not noticed Rogan and that gave Rogan a sense of satisfaction.

Captain Ricsige Brecott was the man chosen by the Sherriff to investigate the murders in Kāldākinn and he was to take with him Sigegar Youngblood as his scribe. the captain was an older man who was formally in the queen's personal bodyguard until recently when he was retired, since then he has been serving with the Sherriff in Ingolfsfell, secretly at the behest of the king.

Rogan observed a man of good character, serious, studious, and firm but fare. Rogan thought that he might be able to confide in this man, and that if he were to be this forth coming, this former Captain of the Royal Guard, might just have knowledge that he did not yet possess.

Outside, Alti signalled to the others and still in secret they followed Rogan and Aatu.

They had been on the road and away from Ingolfsfell about half an hour before the captain began to speak, to Rogan, but not so quietly that some of the others couldn't hear. "You don't much care for our esteemed Sherriff do you Rogan?"

"He's a murdering swine and as corrupt as the day is long, Captain, and he has sent you on a fool's errand, he knows it and I know it."

"Why are you so sure, Rogan?"

"Because on our journey, here we were ambushed by his men and the two we brought to him were later released without charge, and they were responsible for the death of one of my men in that fight."

"What two men do you speak of?"

"Arnvid and Guthorm."

"I hate to be the barer of bad news but both Arnvid and Guthorm are Skuld's men, and I would wager that his father knows little or nothing about who that little urchin is in league with."

"So, you think it could have been Skuld who killed my men at the village?"

"Probably, although Scoppi Hranfast is Magnus's personal bodyguard, I have seen him in secret talking with Skuld plenty of times, and with coin changing hands a plenty."

"So what?"

"Scoppi is an assassin of great repute, if it is as you say, about your guards and the way they died, then it is Scoppi who killed them, and he could easily have carried that out on his own."

"Why are you bothering to come with us if you already suspect that is the case?"

"I'm intrigued, Rogan. I want to know what is really going on, and I may no longer be in the service of the queen, but I am very much in the pay of the king."

9 New Friends

The journey back to Kaldakinn was uneventful and Rogan and his warriors were grateful to be home. brother Cuthbald and Alderman Renwick were both waiting by the open gates to welcome everyone home. Rogan introduced brother Cuthbald to Captain Brecott and his assistant Sigegar and then to Renwick. brother Cuthbald was the only one to question why one who rode out has not returned, but he was greeted with silence by all as they trooped past.

Before anything more that day, Rogan insisted that everyone took time out to rest and eat, Captain Brecott was invited to stay at the manor house with Rogan. While they ate, both men talked about their lives up until the day they met, and both realised that they had the answers to each other's puzzle.

Captain Brecott was relieved of his service to the queen when she announced that she had got a completely new bodyguard made up of the most highly skilled warriors in the Shattered Realms, and all of her previous guards would be relocated to different posts elsewhere in the kingdom. However, before he was posted the king called him to a private meeting with a nun.

Sister Wenyid Tanner had approached the king about the disappearance of possibly hundreds of women from just about every town and village in the kingdom, including from the royal household. Mostly, the women were the sort that weren't missed, drunks, petty thieves, prostitutes and the like, but then it became many women at around the same time including servants to both the king and queen, and it was always women between a certain age, then about five years ago children too began to disappear without any bodies ever being found.

Rogan agreed that these missing people were the ones like himself who ended up with the Orsk in Obreā, but to what end. Ongar had invited himself in and was listening to the conversation before butting in and saying, "That's where I come in!"

Both men beckoned Ongar to the table to eat with them and the captain said, "Please continue."

"The women were taken to produce babies for the Orsk, the Orsk race is dying out and they need us, half-bloods to secure their future, you see they only have one Orsk female in the whole of the kingdom under the mountain, and she is probably the oldest living thing on earth, so that was never going to cut it, the plan was to impregnate human women and to supplement the strength of the half-bloods they would take and teach captured boys like you Rogan to fight with them."

"Ongar is correct, but what I could never work out was why, why do they put half-bloods and humans together?"

"Yes, indeed, to what end?" said the captain.

"It has to have something to do with the Black Guard!" Ongar said.

"How do you know about the Black Guard, Ongar?" the captain inquired.

"That is the name of the half-bloods who don't get rejected like I did, and who move up to living on the top of the mountain in a great castle. Rogan, who do you think we made all those weapons and armour for?"

"Do you think that your Black Guard are the same as the queen's Black Guard, they are all at least six foot and clad all in black leather from head to toe and they wear plate armour when they are on duty, built like stone golems?"

Silence befell the room.

"The question is, what are we going to do about it?" asked Rogan.

"Or, what can we do about it?" stated captain Brecott.

"The queen is setting up garrisons of Black Guards in every city, town and now villagers, what do you both think is going on?" Ongar interjected.

"She is getting ready to seize power from her husband!" said the captain.

"Why stop there, why not seize the whole of the Shattered Realms?" Rogan said wistfully.

"It's no secret that Mårcådiå and Råvenniå have been uneasy bed fellows ever since the queen's brother king Eadweard of Mårcådiå effectively gave her away to marry King Hamund of Råvenniå when she was just fifteen years of age."

"Did you know that Queen Helga and Matilda Steinolf are best friends and that the queen dotes on Æstrid, the daughter she never had!" Brecott added.

"It is all still tenuous to say the least, and it begs the question where are we going with all of this?" mused Rogan.

"I say we round up all the fighters from here to Lāngāholt and attack the Orsk and liberate all the captives, including all the half-bloods, at least then we can stop this vile practice of women and children snatching," offered Ongar.

"Captain Brecott was all in favour of keeping the Royal family out of this as much as they could, fighting on one front would be about as much as they could muster at this time."

"I say we wait, no attacking anyone until we are absolutely sure who is responsible for what, that way we can continue to build a case against those in charge while at the same time learn who could help us should this all get out of hand," said Rogan.

"Aye, lad, I think you are right so now we need to widen our inner circle, but who can we trust?" asked the captain.

"We start with my twelve most trusted bodyguards and include brother Cuthbald and Renwick of course."

"Eleven, Rogan, remember we are one warrior short." Ongar pointed out.

"Hmm, Ricsige, I would be honoured if you joined my warband, and then I think we should speak with Gufi and Arn, I am sure they will support us and if so then we at least have an army of around three hundred."

"Gufi and Arn?" inquired the captain.

"They are the chieftains of Hundsnes and Lāngāholt, and like Rogan I am sure we already have their support in whatever venture we undertake," remarked Ongar.

Brother Cuthbald was the first outside of Rogan's trusted warriors to talk to and he immediately said that they should send for a church warden from Mårcådiå, called Leofstan Ealdwulf, he was a remarkable warrior of God and was able to sniff out a conspiracy in a pile of freshly washed laundry,

172

also Sister Wenyid Tanner, she had her own set of valuable skills, as well as being adept with the sword.

Brenn and Willem both asked if they should try to contact Brenn's father, Chief Eric Wigheard, in Lōrnicā, he could ask the king to raise an army and join them in fighting the Orsk. Rogan said he would bare that in mind, although he wasn't sure if anyone even knew if the two boys were still alive as they would have had no news in the last year or more.

Aethelric wondered if they should actually send a delegation to both neighbouring realms, Fōrren and Lōrnicā as it was most likely they too had lost people to this insidious plot.

Ingrid asked if they were any point in including Jarl Sigfusson in on what they were talking about, but Ricsige Brecott rebutted that idea immediately, "He is a lap dog of Matilda Steinolf and therefore of no use whatsoever."

"Right here is the plan, Ongar, Ingrid, Halla and the captain will come with me to Ingolfsfell to look for Sister Wenyid, Aethelric you will take Brenn, Willem, Zaryi and Nariako to Lōrnicā, that leaves, Gunnar, Olpaz, Soiveig, Atli and Sigrunn to make their way to Fōrren."

Sigegar Youngblood was to stay with brother Cuthbald in Kāldākinn and you can travel to Hundsnes and Lāngāholt to report some of what we have talked about to Gufi and Arn, but being careful how much you divulge.

"Brother Cuthbald, how do you propose we get a message to Leofstan Ealdwulf?" Rogan asked.

"I will send a message via ecumenical means, don't worry it will be very discrete."

It was agreed that the four parties would stagger their leaving times so as not to draw unwanted attention and their

173

individual back stories for family and friends was that they were simply going out to investigate new land as the village is rapidly expanding and suitable sites need to be located.

Aethelric and his party slipped away first as they had the longest journey to make to Lōrnicā, and half an hour later it was the turn of Gunnar's party to make their way to Fōrren. After another half hour, Rogan set out for Ingolfsfell. Brother Cuthbald would follow shortly afterwards as he had the shortest journey to make to the two sister villages.

Aethelric the bard was intelligent, articulate, and if Ongar was Rogan's right-hand man, then Aethelric was his left-hand man. and the cover story that his party would be using to hide their real purpose was to be that they were part of a group of wandering entertainers who were looking for new places to find work.

Aethelric could play a wide selection of instruments and sing many different songs from bawdy ale house to ones fit for the ears of royalty, Brenn and Willem, just until they found the chief, were to be jugglers however, because of their constant mistakes in training it was thought that they could actually be jesters and the mistakes could be worked in as part of their act.

Zaryi was brilliant at throwing knives and hitting her target precisely, so that would be her cover as a knife thrower, and Nariako was a superb shot with a bow, and her trick was to stand a piece of fruit on one of the boy's heads and split it in half with an arrow from one hundred paces.

By horse and at a canter, the journey as far as the turn in the road to Hundsnes took nine hours and they covered a little over eighteen leagues, when they stopped for a short brake, Aethelric would take this time to search the hedge rows for

174

herbs and mosses for Solveig to use in her medicine making, while the others practiced at their new professions as travelling entertainers.

By the time they had travelled the five leagues to Lāngāholt, it was around mid-afternoon and Aethelric decided that it was only polite to enter the village and speak with Chief Arn Sigewulfsson.

Arn listened to the news from Aethelric with guarded enthusiasm, adding that once brother Cuthbald had been and confirmed Aethelric's story he would join in with whatever preparations he could without endangering his village and his people.

Aethelric had asked for advice regarding the journey to Lōrnicā and he wanted to know what sort of people they were, Brenn and Willem's help had stretched as far as, "Everything will be fine, just let us do the talking." Zaryi was from a realm far to the southwest called Tålåmårå and Nariako was from even further to the south, across the Dark Water Channel and a land called Ascomanni, so neither of them had any idea of what lay ahead.

Arn said that he would send some of his warband to guide them to an inland river that formed part of western border between Fōrren and Råvenniå called the Tawa River, from there they could hire a fishing boat that could take them all the way to the top edge of Fōrren were the river splits in two, the east branch would take them all the way into Lōrnicā.

Arn asked if they would like to rest a while longer as the journey from here to the fishing settlement of Heeshem, Arn would give them a written letter baring his seal and some coins with which to pay for the hiring of a boat. That much the Chief said was the least that he could do at this time. After a short break, Aethelric's party was on the move, and for the next six hours they had an escort of twelve of Arn's household Guard.

When they had arrived at the settlement of Heeshem, Arn's mounted guard wished them every success and departed for their home village leaving the five of them to ask about a boat and to be convincing with their stories. The people from the settlement numbered around one hundred and twenty and they were of a wide range in age, from tiny babes to very old ones.

The leader of the village was a man who identified himself as Elder Deowuc, and from first impressions his village looked like it was just about holding on, surprisingly when they were offered hospitality, just about every dish contained fish, cheese and malt bread, there was a distinct absence of red meat, or even white meat, they drank mead and didn't even brew ale.

While at first the Elder was sceptical of their reason for being there and wanting to hire a boat, watching Brenn and Willem put on jester's costumes and attempt to juggle anything had him convinced that they truly were fools and therefore harmless, Aethelric though insisted on putting on a proper show and he said to the Elder, there would be no cost, it would be given in exchange for the settlement's hospitality.

Zari asked the watching people to give her ideas on what she could throw her knives at, and she told them not to make the suggestions easy. One little boy stepped forward and asked if she could really hit a piece of fruit on a person's head, and she asked for a volunteer so that she could demonstrate that she could.

At first, nobody was courageous enough to step forward and so she scanned the faces of her audience until she found a man who looked like he enjoyed bragging about his prowess as a warrior, there was always one in every town or village and this man was no exception.

Zaryi began her routine by buttering the man up and once she was confident that she had her 'mark' she got him to agree, albeit under protest, to go and stand over by an almond-scented hagberry tree with its smooth greyish-brown bark.

"Tell me, what is your name?"

"Betlic!"

"Excellent now we know what to inscribe on your grave!"

>Laughter<

"Betlic, I am only kidding, don't worry I have done this many times, even blindfolded, although I cannot prove what I say as nobody ever survived."

>more laughter<

"All right, I will need a volunteer from the audience to come and place an apple on Betlic's head, I would do it myself but my are shaking terribly."

A young woman came forward to offer her services, and Zaryi could see that she took great pleasure in watch this man suffer, although not to the extent that she wished Zaryi to miss.

"Now once you have placed the apple on Betlic's head, please stand well back for your own safety, in fact stand behind me for your own safety."

"I really don't think you should be attempting this Zaryi, please can you choose someone else?"

"Oh, you don't want these people to think you a coward do you, I mean what could possibly go wrong, now I need you to spread out your arms and stand with your legs apart."

"Are you sure about this?"

"Yes, you will be perfectly fine if you stand completely still, like your life depended on it, which it probably does."

"I am not so sure about this can I at least have some time to think about it?"

Zaryi threw the first of eleven small knives, and it struck the tree right between Betlic's legs, just below his crouch. Which made Betlic yelp in shock.

"Oh, don't worry I was aiming for the apple on the head, stay still I will try again."

The next knife struck on the right side of his leg just below the knee.

"Hmm, my aim is a little off today, let me have another couple of warm up throws and I will get the apple, I promise." The next throw hit above the knee and to the right.

"I know I should try and stand a little more to the left." Then two more throws one below the knee and to the left and another above the knee, then in very quick succession, one, two. Three, four more knives, one above each outstretched arm and one below each arm.

By now, poor Betlic was paralysed with fear and the audience were hushed in awe and expectation.

"Ah ha, I know what the problem is, do you know what the problem is?" she asked Betlic, but he did not dare answer or move.

"The problem is you, sir, you look so scared that you are making me nervous, I know just the thing." And she scanned the audience looking for her next prop, and she saw an older

178

man wearing a neckerchief, and she asked if she could borrow it for a moment.

After tying it around her head so that she could not see Betlic, she said, "That is much better." And she turned away from Betlic and faced the opposite direction.

"Where is Betlic?" she asked the audience.

"He's behind you!" they shouted excitedly, not daring to believe that she would throw her last knife blindfolded.

'Thunk!' She threw that last knife and it wedged into the tree solidly, right above Betlic's head, splitting the apple perfectly in two, and the crowd of people were delighted and applauded vigorously, all except Betlic who was still praying to the gods of the woodlands and a few others besides. When Betlic was told he could step away from the tree, there was left behind a perfect shape of him with the knives.

Nariako was an expert archer and for her 'trick', she asked for three volunteers from the audience to come and stand in front of her near to the tree, then she gave them each an apple and stepped back twenty paces which she counted out loudly and to which some of those watching began to join in.

"Now, will the first person throw their apple as high in the air as possible." And she was able to mount an arrow and fire it straight through the middle of the apple before it had completed its decent, and she had the other two repeat what the first had done before giving them each another apple.

"And for my next demonstration, I want all tree of you to throw your apples high into the air at the same time." And as they did, she let loose two arrows that pierced two of the apples in quick succession, but the third she purposely allowed to fall and her third arrow she fired, hit the fruit just above the last persons head, and once more the crowd applauded gleefully.

Aethelric and the others were invited to be guests of honour at that evenings communal meal, and it was then that Aethelric demonstrated his fine talents, first by playing a beautiful melody on his lyre, and then by singing a couple of truly sweet songs, his voice changing pitch in such a manner as to enchant the audience completely, and then as the mead flowed, his songs descended into those that would have only graced an ale house, however they were all the songs the settlers would join in with.

Later that evening, the settlement Elder had introduced Aethelric to a boat master who said that he would gladly navigate them up the Tawa River and into Lōrnicā and after some coins had changed hands the journey by boat began.

The fisherman spoke a heavily accented version of Ingolandic with some unusual local touches which made communication nigh on impossible, which led Aethelric to ask if there were anyone available who could translate, and a young boy was plucked from the arms of a local women and plonked unceremoniously in the boat with the rest of them.

They group put their part of the mission into the hands of a stranger who they could neither understood them, nor did they understand him, apart from the name of the realm they were heading towards, Lōrnicā.

The old man spoke with the boy, and the boy said that with the wind against the sail they should be prepared to be on the water for about fifteen hours even though the distance is about the same as from here back to Lāngāholt, he says there is a storm brewing up north and they would run head first into it at Fōrren point, so they were to be ready to pitch in and do as the old man said or be sunk, explained the boy with a smile and a sense of satisfaction that he had covered everything the old man had said.

"Great, so we can't understand a word he is saying but we might have to do everything he says, if we are to survive this journey?"

"Yes, pretty much!"

"Well, it was nice knowing you all my friends!" Willem forlornly said.

What the fisherman had neglected to mention was that with the wind against them and therefore a useless sail, they would all have to pitch in and row, Brenn and Willem lasted about one hour until they no longer had the strength to row, the fisherman bellowed something to them through the ever-increasing wind and light rain which sounded like rest.

They did not need a translator to tell them to up oars and find space in the bottom of the boat to rest. Zaryi and Nariako found the rhythm of the others who were rowing and soon found that they were competing against each, first to outlast the boys which they did easily and then to give the other a run for their money.

Aethelric missed the odd pull but otherwise like the shield maidens did not want to give up to soon and appear to lose face, the other men gave grudging cheers as the vessel cut through the water with relative ease and gave the wind no chance to push it back.

By the time the boat had reached the mouth of the river where it separated left towards Lōrnicā and straight ahead to a great expanse of water which led to the open sea, Aethelric realised that they were at the crossing point from where they escaped the orcs. "Look, boys, look where we are do you recognise this place?" both shouted against the wind that they did indeed and their hearts leaped because they both shouted that they knew the way home from here.

At that moment, a large gust of wind hit the boat and it lurched heavily to the east and the rugged shoreline of Fōrren, the fisherman shouted something incomprehensible, and his men began to row hard as he turned the rudder towards the riverbank. "Look, he is telling us to do something and to be quick about it," shouted Zaryi. "Raise the main sail I think, look how he gestures towards it."

So, the five helped to haul the main sail up to the top of its mast and as the boat lurched one more time the sail caught the wind and she was off at a handsome rate of knots, but this time down the left fork in the river and towards Lōrnicā. Eventually, the boat came to another small fishing village, this time in Lōrnicā, which Brenn called, Ramscliff, probably due to the number of sheep that littered the cliff side just to the east of the beach where the village lay.

Aethelric paid a little more coin to the fisherman and patted him goodbye on his shoulder and the group climbed out and on to the sand in search of someone in authority.

10 A Fool's Errand

Gunnar Helgisson and his party had fallen about an hour behind Aethelric's party by the time they had met with Chief Arn and then been escorted to the small fishing settlement of Heeshem, it did not matter now because they just wanted passage across the river and for that purpose there was a simple pull-rope ferry so no questions needed to be asked and the escort did not need to go all the way to the ferry with them which might have drawn suspicions so soon after the other party had left.

The ferry was a large wide raft roped together with a raised wooden floor to keep the water off the passengers' feet. It was guided across the water by a team of horses either side and two ropes that went through hoops attached to the raft in each of the four corners, a steersman would then work a paddle to make sure that the raft didn't drift to much while being pulled forward across the river. The journey took about an hour and during that time Gunnar kept his own company while Atli and Sigrunn acted like two young love birds who couldn't keep their hands off each other and the other two, Solveig and Olpaz who tried to look happy being together but who unintentionally drew attention to themselves by their Icey body language.

Back when they were all captives Solveig had given birth to her first baby not being much older than her fifteenth year, the birth had been terribly painful and the baby which it was whispered was a girl was taken away from her never to be seen again, and that was why she had a strong hatred for the Orsk.

Olpaz, for his part was probably the worst at everything that it was possible to be, he stood a gangly five feet eight but his demur was most awkward, he had no muscle what so ever, his stomach and chest was sucked in while his head, pelvis and nobbily knees all stuck out, and he was last teammate to get picked and in the case of the tournament, the first to be eliminated.

He followed Solveig everywhere as she was the only one who ever gave in any time, but she was resentful and cruel to him, but he was like a lovesick puppy, he just kept coming right back. He was a useless with a sword as he was with a bow and the only weapon, he did seem to be able to handle well was a club, and when Rogan was able to put his hands on a proper war hammer that had a flat bashing end and a hooked claw on the other, Olpaz was delighted and he really seemed to come out of his shell a bit more.

Once the ferry had crossed the river and the party were ashore, they were immediately approached by guards from the local garrison in Axley, the village on the opposite bank. A troop of fourteen soldiers lined up either side of them and a captain, who introduced himself as, Pàrlan Breac, came forward and asked them individually, for their names and what their business was, and how long they intended to stay.

Breac was by far and away the most colourful of any soldier Gunnar had met to date, he wore a full length white frock-tunic, whose skirt was in like strips, on top of this he wore chainmail but it was cut at the waist, his helmet was iron and so where his knee length leg grieves, and he carried a large oval shield which was painted white with a red outer rim and a cross motive across its centre.

Gunnar Helgisson introduced himself first and said that he had come from Råvenniå on important business on behalf of the king of Råvenniå, Hammund Arnbjorg and that it was imperative that he speak with someone at the court of King Weagstan Godhelm. To back up his diplomatic mission, he produced a letter written by Captain Brecott of the king's household guard.

"Well, I have no doubt that your mission is of grave concern to you my Lord Helgisson so I will escort you to the capital myself, whether you can gain an audience with the king is above my station however, I will take you directly to someone who may be able to help."

Gunnar introduced Atli and Sigrunn and said that they were his companions on this mission, he made no mention of Solveig and Olpaz as they were to report back to Rogan if anything happened to the other three, if the purpose of their visit was not given to the king.

Solveig had insisted on bring her pigeon with her on this mission and finally she had found a use for Olpaz, he was the pigeon's new keeper, and was to take it everywhere that Solveig went, which of course meant that now he had a real job and a real reason to be at Solveig's side. *The keeper of the pigeon*, Olpaz repeated those words over and over again in his mind.

There was just one little thing, that he dare not mention to Solveig about the pigeon for fear that she might react badly, if she knew, and that was that, well the pigeon didn't always look the same. The thought had crossed Olpaz's mind that the bird might be enchanted and even if it was, did Solveig already know about it, he thought that he would mention it to Rogan when next they met.

The journey from the ferry to the capitol city, which was four leagues away would take approximately one hour as they were all mounted. Förren was a fraction of the size of Råvenniå and very sparsely populated so what were great distances back home were but short trips here.

The capitol was not at all what Gunnar had expected it to be like, it was oblong in shape and was possibly only slightly larger than Kāldākinn, it had high wooden walls and was perched atop of a flattened hill, but on the right side of the wall in the very corner there was a tall three story building which was square and quite clearly made from wattle and daub and then painted white in order to weather proof it, but Gunnar didn't doubt that he could probably kick an hole right through it with a couple of swift movements of his foot.

Once they had passed through the outer gate house which was a spacious oblong box (again) that resembled an oblong house built on top of the gate top, from a short distance outside Olpaz and Solveig followed Gunner and the other two, Atli and Sigrunn as much as they could without drawing attention to themselves.

It was at this point that Solveig suddenly announced that it would be better if they split up, 'just in case'.

Olpaz wondered out loud, "Just in case, what?" But Solveig feigned that Gunnar was going out of their line of sight and they needed to act quickly, and without waiting for his reply, she snatched the basket with pigeon in it and disappeared in to the crowd.

Olpaz said he would wait where he was until she came back for him, but he realised by this time that he was in fact talking to himself, she was long gone.

Half an hour later, Olpaz caught sight of the captain returning with someone who was of high rank indeed, the newcomer wore a white linen tunic under a beautifully crafted leather top which its self-lay on top of finely linked chainmail, dress chainmail as it was far too delicate to wear in battle, then he recognised the man.

But he admitted to himself that he easily forgot things he was supposed to remember and remembered things that he should have easily forgot, this man though, who stood around five feet five with jet black hair and with a receding front hairline, and a permanent scowl was, piercing eyes, someone he should have known, it was on the tip of his tongue, Tostig Seaward!

Solveig was nowhere to be seen at first and Olpaz began to panic, fortunately the two men had stridden confidently by without noticing Olpaz and just as he turned to follow them, he caught sight of Solveig and sighed with relief.

Olpaz opened his mouth to say something important but just like that he noticed that the pigeon wasn't in the basket anymore that Solveig was still carrying, and so he forgot what it was he was going to say, and instead asked where the bird had gone.

"Olpaz! Am I glad to see you, I thought that you would follow me and so imagine my shock when I did turn about and you were no longer there, in my haste I dropped the basket and the pigeon flew off, oh but I was far more worried about you, dear sweet Olpaz." And as she was almost upon him, she opened her arms wide, with which to tenderly hold him, much like a mother would greet one of her lost offspring, once they had been found.

Olpaz might have been considered slow by those that knew him but he recognised a hug when he saw one, and so he reciprocated the gesture not daring to miss this opportunity for the world, in point of fact in his mind this was the moment that he had wished for since first he set eyes on Solveig Arnulfrid.

She did indeed hold him tight to her, and he basked in every second of it and he thought that if this were to be his last moment of this earth then it was worth savouring, it had been but a second since they embraced that Olpaz felt a most unusual sensation in his stomach and at first, he had no idea what it could be, other than it was painful and the more the pain grew the more he needed to separate from Solveig and see what was causing it, but she held on to him even more tightly than before and he recalled hearing her whispering something in his ear, but those words, whatever they were became a distant sound, and he felt himself cough, he was having trouble breathing.

Finally, Solveig was releasing her grip on him, and he began to feel himself slipping out of her grasp and he looked for the first time longingly in her eyes and he didn't understand, when he coughed once more why the sticky red liquid was pouring from his mouth.

Solveig retracted the needle-sharp blade from his stomach and wiped it on his tunic as Olpaz slumped back against the wall and began to slide down it and on to the ground. His body had slid into a sitting position with his knees up and Solveig gently placed his bowed head on his knees and Olpaz breathed his last breath before embracing the cold darkness of eternity.

Solveig quickly stepped away from the dead half-breed, made sign with her right hand and continued to follow in the direction the captain, Atli, Sigrunn and Gunnar had gone, and although she had lost sight of them, she knew that they were all heading to the palace.

The market area was full of people and plenty of soldiers and Solveig needed to put some distance between herself and the body so far only a handful of other people knew who she was and one of them she had only met once in Ingolfsfell, the other three were on their way to the castle.

But if the three thought that the good people would warmly welcome them then they were sadly mistaken, because the captain took them through a series of check points before letting them in through a large wooden door which he opened but insisted that they go in first, only to slam that door shut behind them.

Gunnar Atli and Sigrunn sat on a wooden bench in a room made of stone which had straw strewn about it and chains and shackles hanging from spikes that had been driven in to the walls and floor, watching and waiting, for someone to do or say something for what seemed like an eternity.

The large heavy door to the room squealed on its hinges as it was pushed open, the waft of fresh air was a change to the foul-smelling room, Captain Pàrlan Breac had returned with a young well-dressed man who he introduced as his Royal Highness Prince Tostig Godhelm of Fōrren.

Gunnar raised himself from his bench and bowed slightly and the other two followed his example, then the two men looked at each other and smiled. "Well at least they teach you manners wherever you are from, Gunnar, is it?"

"Yes, Gunnar Helgisson, and I have important information from Råvenniå, from my lord chief Rogan Ragisson and a signed letter with the seal of the captain of the royal household guard and the seal of the king himself."

"The king of Råvenniå, then this must be pressing business indeed, but this is not the place that we should discuss these matter's perhaps we shall find a quiet room at the palace, come Gunnar Helgisson, and you two as well, it would appear we have much to discuss, Pàrlan, I can take it from here. Please return to your duties, oh and one other thing Gunnar?"

"Yes, Lord Prince?"

"Did you three come together or were there more of you, it is not important either way I am just curious as to how important this message really is for just one man and what, only two guards, to convey it, you understand, no?"

"I am do, we did have two other companions who were watching from a distance, once they knew that we had made contact, their role in this mission was over, so as we speak they are probably halfway home by now."

"Ah, I see, and a very clever answer that, Gunnar, very clever."

The prince waved his hand and all of the guards in sight suddenly disappeared through doors leaving the four of them alone. "So, tell me of all your plans concerning this matter, I take it that it isn't as straight forward as just asking if we could send you some soldiers to fight in a distant battle at some date in the future, surely not, tell me that I am confused or wrong."

Gunnar told the prince that he had pretty much got the gist of it but then he asked, "So what do you think, will the king help us, or not?"

"Hmm, we will see, but first we had better go and see if my father will grant us an audience, he is very old and very, very cranky these days, so don't worry if he doesn't want to see you today because I am sure that he will eventually."

Tostig took them to a room off a long straight corridor that stank of polished wood and their foot falls clomped and echoed off the walls, until they reached the room that Tostig had said would be private. "In here, if you please. Now before we get down to business, is there anything I can get you, food or a drink perhaps?"

Tostig raised his right arm and clicked his fingers once in the empty room and as if by magic a servant appeared from a door that didn't look like a door until it was open, Gunnar was impressed.

"I haven't eaten all day, and a drink would be most welcome, thank you, Lord Prince."

"Not at all, if what you have told me is true then I think you and I are going to be seeing a lot more of each other."

The servant returned from the concealed room with a platter of hot food whose centre piece was a full roast chicken, and then he returned with tree large silver tankards of ale, which as each of his guests took hold of before the prince banged with his crystal, jewel encrusted goblet, with them all, "Skoll!"

For the next hour or so, Gunnar had to repeat the story that he had been given to memory by Rogan, because the prince had called for it all to be written down for legal reasons while continually calling for everyone's tankards to be re-filled.

It took another hour or so before Gunnar, who was feeling quite disorientated, paused to await the prince's response. The prince said that he would send for the king's chamberlain, he would be the person who would know if women and children were going missing in Forren. Although the prince did say there and then that he hadn't heard anything about this sort of thing from any quarter.

Gunnar belched and said, "This very fortunate for you, Lord Prince, and for the women and children of this realm!" It was evident that Gunnar was drunk by now and right where the prince had wanted him.

Solveig, Atli and Sigrunn had already fallen into a deep sleep.

Gunnar managed to keep mumbling to no one in particular for at least another ten minutes before he too succumbed to sleep.

The following day, the prince crossed paths with his father the king of Fōrren, and the king asked where his son had been all evening, the prince waved away the conversation saying, "Oh you know me, Father, if there is a gathering to be had then I simply mustn't refuse, it would be impolite."

"Free drink and plenty of wenches I hope!"

"Of course, father, we have our reputations to keep up."

"Nothing I should know about Tostig?"

"No, dear Father, now stop fretting I have a frightful headache!"

The king laughed as he walked away.

Gunnar awoke with a head that felt like it had been trapped in a vice, and as he slowly opened his eyes, he found it hard to comprehend just exactly where he was, it was cold, dark and stank like an open sewer.

"Ah, finally, I thought you were going to sleep all day!" said the voice from the figure who hung back in the shadows.

"Where am I, and what have you done with my friends?"

"Now, the way this works best, is if you let me ask the questions, and you just stay quiet until I need you to speak, how does that sound?"

"Wait, are those bars, am I in some sort of cell?"

"Oh dear, you're not listening," said the voice and just then from somewhere else in the shadows someone launched the contents of a bucket threw the bars at Gunnar.

The icy water bit at Gunnar's exposed skin, for then he realised that he had been stripped down to his under garments., and he was about to protest when he checked himself.

"That's better, you're a quick learner after all, good, shall we start with your name and where you are from?"

The questioning went on for ages and Gunnar was having trouble keeping conscious enough to answer all the questions.

"Who is taking the women and children?"

"The Orsk!"

"Why are they taking them?"

"To build an army."

"Why do they want to build an army?"

"I don't know."

"Did you come here with any other people?"

"Yes, but I haven't seen them since last night."

"Where there any others?"

"Yes, I have already told the prince, there were two but they are long gone."

"Was one of your friends a half-breed?"

"Yes! Olpaz, why have you found him, is he here?"

"We found him all right, left in the market area, dead!"

"Dead! Who killed him, is this part of some elaborate hoax, why would anyone want to kill him?"

"I rather hoped you could tell me, if he was your friend, or was he following you and you killed him?"

"Why would I kill him, it would make no sense."

"It would, if, you are lying and he was indeed one of these so-called abductors of women and children, if you admit this then perhaps, we can clear this all up and you can go free."

"I have told you the truth, as I told the prince last night the truth, I came here with letter's baring the king's seal, you must believe me, or we could all be in danger."

"Yes, yes, yes, so you keep saying, we are in danger from whom though, really?"

"I don't know, from whoever is building an army."

"I think I understand, you want an army from Fōrren to march out to Obreā and fight these Orsk who are building an army and while we slip out of our country, what will happen, perhaps Rogan will appear with an army of his own and poof, a wide-open country for him to take for himself or for the king who gave you his Royal seal?"

At that very moment, the door to dimly lit corridor was thrown open and a torch was poked through into the darkness.

"What on earth is going on down here and why wasn't I informed!" shouted a voice that sounded familiar to Gunnar.

It was the prince, and he strode over to the other voice who had been asking all the questions, and in the glow of the torch Gunnar watched as the prince slapped the interrogator across the face.

"Imbecile! Open the cell door, this man is an honoured guest!"

"Yes, my lord prince, I am sorry."

The door was opened, and Gunnar helped to his feet and brought to the prince.

"Please accept my most sincere apologies for this terrible, terrible misunderstanding, but after you disappeared last night, I was out looking for you with half the palace guard but you were nowhere to be found until I overheard two guards talking about a dead body and a foreigner who was being questioned about his death."

Gunnar couldn't remember anything, but he knew with every muscle and sinew in his body that he wouldn't have hurt Olpaz let alone kill him.

The prince took Gunnar to the same room that they had been in the previous night and where Atli and Sigrunn were waiting eagerly to find out what happened themselves, the prince asked his servant again to bring food and perhaps just water to drink. It was hard for Gunnar not to be embarrassed and truly grateful to the prince and his untimely rescue.

"Well, while you were out on your little adventure in my city all night, I found out some information about what we talked about, some women and children have been reported as going missing without a body ever turning up, but thankfully for us, nothing on the scale you have been talking about, in fact less than a hundred across the whole country in the last ten years, but whatever the true figure, it is too many to go unpunished, so what is it you are proposing we do about it?"

"One proposal would be for each realm to send into Obreā an army like the world has never seen before and hopefully never will again and together we will attack the Orsk in their cave villages, and freeing any prisoners we find, but putting to death any who stand in our way."

"And you believe, or the king's man, this er, captain Brecott, believes that together our combined forces would be enough?"

"Well, honestly no, we don't have any idea of how many Orsk live in those wretched villages."

11 An Unexpected Journey

Rogan's journey to Ingolfsfell was quite uneventful this time around which was welcome as Rogan had split half of his trusted warriors into three groups and he was now travelling the other eleven of them, including Captain Brecott but not Aatu. Aatu came along whether he had been invited or not.

There was no pretense this time either as everybody who was anybody already knew Captain Ricsige Brecott and, there was even a tale or two springing up around Rogan and his white dog with different coloured eyes, as Aatu was becoming known, which wasn't far from the truth as a warg was a type of wolf and all dogs came originally from wolves, just far more intelligent and savage.

On the way to the sheriff's house, it was agreed that they would tell him everything they had found out, except anything that was either to connected with the sheriff's family or the queen, the plan had been all along to blame this on the Orsk, entirely.

Rogan needed an army and to get that army he would need to tell such a tale, one that could pull everyone together even if they were a hundred here and a hundred there, all those hundreds would add up. However, the mere whiff of anything but Orsk involvement, and people would start to be suspicious of each other and the whole plan would collapse.

The five companions halted their horses outside the sheriff's house and tied them to one of the two long posts that sat outside the building, the last time Rogan had been here was to have those two murdering cures interned, what ever happened to them Rogan never found out, and before he could think on it anymore, he became distracted by a low flying bird that had just swooped past and seemed to have flow right into the sheriff's house.

"Did I just imagine that or did anyone else just see a bird fly right into this very building?"

But before anyone could answer there came another distracting sound, their attention was quickly drawn to some muffled noises over in the large barn, where prisoners were kept in cages awaiting judgement.

Rogan could not believe his eyes, for the second time in as many minutes, these two birds were in fact, Arnvid Hammerfell and Guthorm Brondulfsson, and they were lost in horseplay teasing each other over something or nothing.

But you know when you have one of those moments when the hairs on the back of your neck stand up, when you think that someone is looking at you, well that was just the feeling that those two criminals had when they looked up and saw Rogan with eleven of his most trusted warriors and Aatu who was now twice the size that he was, they bolted down the side of the long barn and out of sight.

Aatu growled and was about to sprint after them and even Rogan was about to mount up and give chase, Captain Brecott checked him, and Aatu, telling him to suck it up, they were murdering scum, but small fry murderers who could be rounded up later. For the time being, they had bigger fish to land.

Magnus came outside to greet the captain and merely nodded to each of the others in turn and in no particular order, "Back so soon Ricsige, and you have managed to keep your horse I see!"

"Good morrow, Magnus, yes, we are back because we have a problem."

"Oh! And what is that problem, nothing to serious I hope, but with so many men at your side, I wonder if I should be worried?"

"Orsk!"

"Orsk?" asked the sheriff sounding genuinely taken aback, as in truth at first sight he could have been forgiven for thinking these men were here for his hide.

"Yes, although all of the bodies had been removed by the time I had arrived, I could see from the way their blood had been spilt on the ground that they had indeed been so brutally murdered by Orsk raiders, perhaps in return for the losses that Rogan had inflicted upon them, or perhaps it had nothing to do with Rogan, and they merely tried to raid the village of Kāldākinn before the alarm was heard."

"How do you know that for sure?"

"Well, yes. As I said, the bodies were not there when I arrived, they had been buried and so I had to look all around the crime scene to discover the truth. The blood patterns told me that first the men were incapacitated and then they were killed one by one afterwards, and it was all carried out under the cover of darkness, it was simple rely. Orsk, everything pointed to them."

"Orsk from Obreā, they are the most likely of all the bits of evidence I put together, they waited and waited and waited some more, over a year, again another fact, for their revenge, and besides sheriff the injuries I had described to me were just not possible to have been done by human hand, no it had to be a monster, or monster, you, see?"

"Yes of course, and why not, they had a score to settle with Rogan and his warriors like you deduced, and that is precisely what they did."

"Well, I can't say it wasn't expected, and I did try to warn everyone involved, but would they listen, and so here we are it was all just about the timing of it, a little over a year late?"

Secretly, the sheriff was sceptical, he wanted it to be just so, the Orsk were a soft target, but he felt they were not being entirely truthful, did he detect for himself a veiled threat or an accusation of some sort?

Scoppi appeared out of the shadow of the inside of the doorway, cleaning the dirt from beneath his fingernails with a long-bladed dagger that glinted every time it was twisted towards the early morning sunrise. A long-bladed dagger just exactly like Ricsige had told Rogan that his men had been killed with, when they spoke in confidence back in Kāldākinn.

"Please, all of you come inside, we have things to discuss, am I right in thinking you will want to exact revenge on these killers? Come now I have said it before and I will say it again, it is what you pay your taxes for."

Rogan looked at Ricsige, not expecting that reply, in fact they had concocted a story so fantastic that it was actually believable, and the sheriff must have been on their wavelength because he just straight up offered them what they thought that they would have to fight tooth and nail for.

"We must go straight to the Jarl, I think if we are to track these monsters down then we are going to need a small army, perhaps even ask our neighbours for help, what do you gentlemen think?"

What these gentlemen thought was that the sheriff must have known their plan all along and was either aiding them now to profit in coin or power, or he had a plan of his own which they were all ensnared in, neither scenario was good because the sheriff was already one step ahead of them either way.

"Forgive me, Sheriff, but the Jarl doesn't seem like a man of action are you sure he will want help us?" asked Rogan, whose mind was going over different scenarios ten to the dozen.

"Of course, he will want to help, your village is his village remember!" the sheriff said quoting directly what the Jarl had said at their last meeting.

Rogan noted that all of the guards were happy to let his large party just waltz in to the castle, with the sheriff, and not so much as raise an eye brow, however, they did insist that most of the men don't go in to see the Jarl, in case he thought that you had come to depose him.

At this meeting, the Jarl did not seem himself, he was distracted and pensive, but he heard what the captain had to say and then sought council as he always did with the sheriff before making his judgement.

"Fetch a scribe! We must record everything in writing." And so, they waited until a scribe was brought from an adjoining room.

"Captain Brecott, I am putting you in charge of this expedition. You will need to send envoys to both Fōrren and to Lōrnicā, they must be persuaded to attack Obreā on three fronts and with a combined army of not less than a thousand warriors, how does that sound?"

"It sounds very generous my lord, and I am sure that three thousand men will bring the required outcome, but I must tell you that we, I, have already taken the liberty of dispatching envoys and even now we are awaiting their return, your grace."

"Impudent or intelligent, Sheriff, what do you say?"

"Most intelligent, my lord, most intelligent, just the reason why I suggested the captain in the first place, he is sure to bring us victory!"

"Who-rah! Gentlemen, who-rah!"

Rogan, the captain and the sheriff all bowed and backed away and out of the room.

"Well, that was remarkably easy," said the captain to nobody in particular.

It was just as the two groups were about to split up, the captain and Rogan to return to Kāldākinn and the sheriff to his house when a particularly well-dressed individual came running up to Captain Brecott. "Edmun Faulkner, is that really you?"

"Oh, yes my lord captain 'tis I, faithful servant of the king, and I have an urgent message that you must drop everything and come with me!"

"All right, it sounds serious, but we will need a little time to prepare ourselves for the journey ahead."

"I have coin for which to pay for fresh horses and food, we are to take extra horses and just swap over when the need arises, now please let us make haste."

The sheriff wasn't expecting any heartfelt goodbyes, so he just casually waved and went inside his house. Hidden out of sight was Skuld and Scoppi, who just inched back from the large doorway of the barn, but close enough to hear what was said before Rogan, Ongar, Halla, Ingrid, the captain, and all of the other, Aatu as well, set off on with Edmun Faulkner to see the king.

Østergård, was the name of the capital of Råvenniå and it lay a little over twenty-eight leagues to the south, a journey on horseback that would take eight hours without stops. Which would give the group plenty of time to talk about just what happened with the sheriff and the Jarl.

Riding further south, Rogan had chance to see a lot more breath-taking sights than he had seen to date, for example, the Straightway pinewoods, so called because they grow either side of the great northern road, which rather confusingly they are travelling south on. There were so many other things to see like the rare species called, Creeping Lady's Tresses, Twinflower and the One-flowered Wintergreen. What about the Tufted Saxifrage, White Mountain Catchfly, Sword-leaved Helleborine, Várgolundur Sandwort, Dark-red Helleborine, Ice king's purslane, Small Cow-wheat and Yellow Oxytropis, to name but a few.

Sadly, all of these beautiful sights were but a distraction from the real conversation they all knew that they should be having. As the true leader of the expedition, Rogan broke the silence. "I don't know how but they are on to us, not everything, but enough, it's giving me a real bad feeling."

"I don't see how they could, we have not discussed this plan outside of my trusted Gedriht," said Rogan.

"As well as Renwick, the priest and Gufi and even Arn Sigewulfsson," Halla added.

"I hate to be the one to say it then Rogan, but we have a spy in our camp!" replied Ongar.

"A spy or just one of us getting to drunk and not being able to hold our tongues?"

"It amounts to the same, doesn't it?" Offered Ingrid.

"We can rule out most of the ones you mentioned Halla because they would actually only just be finding out about the numbers of men we intend to raise, and the Jarl blurted out the exact figures and if you noticed the sheriff was taken aback, either by his graces loose lips or by the fact that he didn't even know the specific number himself."

"Well, that's that then, Rogan, it has to be some one that we have sent out to Lōrnicā or Fōrren. After all, we are all here and paired off, if one person would be doing things out of character then don't you think that one of us would know by now, what about Aatu, doesn't he have a nose for all of this?"

"It simply doesn't stack up, I mean how can they know about some parts of our plan if we are actually the only ones who know about them, those of us who are here now?"

Silence followed that last comment from Halla.

As they continued on their journey down the Great South Road, a road that was built using fine cut stone blocks many hundreds of years before, perhaps by a race of giants, who knows, they decided that it had to be someone outside of those who were present, and so began the conversation about every other member of the twelve that weren't here.

Aethelric and Gunnar were both solid friends of all of those present and they were fully committed to returning to the Orsk settlements, rescuing the prisoners, and then stopping the Black Guard breeding program. Brenn and Willem were ruled out because they were still considered young boys without a care in the world and who would have no interest in this level of intrigue. Atli and Sigrunn were so in love that they could barely have time to breath in between all that kissing and canoodling.

"I don't like where this is leading to Rogan, Olpaz is a half-blood who cannot write in any language so that would rule him out, leaving only Solveig, Nariako and Zaryi, all three of my shield maidens, so I hardly call this a definitive investigation," Ingrid retorted angrily.

"What if we start at the beginning and see where that takes us?" suggested the captain.

"We know that the Orsk working alone are not capable of thinking up this whole breeding program, so we need to find out who is really the brains behind it," Rogan said.

"We think that it is the queen of Råvenniå, and she certainly has the coin to back such a venture," added Ongar.

"But we don't have any solid evidence to take to the king," the captain put in.

"Yet!" said Rogan.

"No, but we do know that the king and queen are estranged, I can confirm that," pointed out the captain.

"And we think that she is trying to put together an army?" said Halla.

"And we want to stop what is happening with the Orsk, the kidnapping and rape of all those women!" Ingrid burst out.

Silence again, rape wasn't something any of them wanted to think about.

"I think we should take a break for a while; this looks like a nice place to let the horses eat some forage and we can stretch our legs," the captain said forcefully.

Ingrid was already sobbing as she dismounted and Halla grabbed the reigns of her horse. "Go sit over there, Ingrid. I will tend to the horses and come sit with you."

Captain Brecott looked down at the ground and shuffled his feet this way and that, Rogan looked over at Ingrid but looked quickly away, and Ongar told him to go speak to her.

Rogan wanted to. He had never seen her this way and didn't know what to do, but Ongar insisted through clenched teeth. "Just go over there and see if she is all right!"

"I'd rather face all the Orsk with a blunt knife!" That was all Rogan could muster.

Reluctantly, Rogan walked over and stood above Ingrid who was by now sitting down in the long grass verge at the side of the road, Halla was with her batting flying insects away with her right hand, as she saw Rogan walk over, she patted Ingrid on her arm and stood up to be with Ongar.

"Ingrid, I am sorry if something I said has upset you."

Rogan crouched Infront of Ingrid and looked into her eyes.

"Something you said! My God Rogan do you not see anything?"

Tears welled in her eyes as others streamed down her cheeks.

"See? What is it that I am meant to see, Ingrid?" Rogan spoke softly now.

"You talk about your trusted men, and then you start going through a list of all the men, and say why you trust them implicitly, even the half-bloods, but oh no, when it comes to the women, my shield maidens then they are the ones you don't trust, so it has to be one of them who is the traitor!" Ingrid saw no point in speaking quietly now.

"Ingrid, it's not like that. I promise."

"You promise what? What did you promise? that you will rid the world of all the Orsk. Then what? Who will you start on next?"

"Ingrid where is all this coming from, I thought that you and I—"

"You thought what? That you could take away all the pain in the world too? Do you realise that every female warrior that follows you, does so because you freed them from being raped everyday by one Orsk after another, they would follow you to the ends of the earth and back, and all you can think of, is that one of us is a spy!" Then Ingrid lurched forward and dropped her head into Rogan's chest and began to sob heavily.

"I had no idea, I am sorry. I don't think you would betray me."

"Why not, I am woman, aren't I?" She gulped her voice muffled by Rogan's heavy sheepskin coat.

"But we are." Rogan was finding it hard to say what was really in his heart.

"There you go again, what is it that you think WE are, Rogan Ragisson?" Ingrid now began to beat his right upper body lightly with her left hand, out of sheer frustration.

"Ingrid, when all of this is over, I want to believe that I did it for you, for us."

"Rogan what are you babbling about, what is this, us?" She lifted her head slightly, tears still flowing, her mouth only inches from his.

"I, I am trying to say that I love you!"

"Eh?" Suddenly, the tears stopped and Ingrid was wide eyed.

"Erm!"

"Shut up, you fool, and kiss me!" she demanded, and they embraced for a long time.

"Well, thank goodness that is finally out of the way, I was beginning to wonder if it was ever going to happen," stated Ongar.

Halla just swiped her right hand out and hit Ongar on his right forearm.

"Right, good, now we have got that all out of the way should be get moving again, we still have a way to go," blurted out the captain feeling somewhat flustered.

Rogan helped Ingrid up into her saddle and patted her gently on the leg as she wriggled to get herself comfy. "I meant what I said, Ingrid."

Ingrid held on to the saddles pommel and leant down to whisper into Rogan's ear, "It's Solveig, she is your spy, she hates the Orsk all right but she also hates the half-bloods especially the ones who came with us, they are a constant reminder to us all, about our pasts."

"Oh, good grief I had no idea, but are you sure it is Solveig, Ingrid?"

"Yes, I am sure, Rogan, but promise me one thing, if we do see her again, please find it in your heart to show her some compassion, we have all been through so much pain and torment, Solveig has been through so much, and you know she never got over them taking away her baby."

"Her baby, but why was there something wrong with it, what did they say?"

"They said nothing, but there was a whisper that the baby was a girl, a half-blood female, and that is why they took it away, but none of us really know, and I doubt we ever will."

Østergård, came in to view for the first time, with it gleaming white towers that sparkled like diamond encrusted jewellery, a city built for another age, perhaps it really was built by giants from across the Várgolundur Sea, every original building was built from stone, with tiled roofs to finish them off, inside there were plaster walls with painted frescos, and where the buildings had fallen into disrepute they had been patched with timber, wattle, and daub. Whoever had built these splendid places had taken their skills with them to the grave.

Rogan felt a cold shiver run down his back, he had seen buildings like these before many years ago, and once more he saw the faces of strangers and heard voices that spoke directly to him from the past, but who were they and where are they now, the cut and design of their clothing was different to any that he had seen so far in Råvenniå.

"Rogan, Rogan, are you all right?" asked Ingrid.

"I'm fine, just a daydream on a sunny day with a beautiful girl."

"Should I be jealous of this beautiful girl, Rogan?"

Rogan just smiled; he was trying to take in his incredible surroundings.

The city had a solid stone wall all around it, the precisely cut stone or stones were cemented together, fifteen feet thick and around thirty feet high, in places the wall like some of the houses was in distress and had been patched up with different materials just to plug the gaps and wooden walkways and long wooden posts to take the weight off the repairs.

The population of Østergård was over twenty thousand and apart from an unknown number of Black Guard the city could boast an army of four thousand, cavalry, foot soldiers and militia, they were one of the most formidable cities in all of the Shattered Realms. The city that could boast that it had never fallen to a foreign invader in its entire history.

Captain Brecott was recognised wherever he went and people would actually stop and applaud him even though he now wore no military uniform or trappings, but he still dressed as a nobleman of the city.

Whatever the people thought of his companions was any bodies guess, but thankfully the streets were filled with the sounds of barking dogs or neighing horses, so seeing the not so little white dog, sat astride Rogan's horse with him, brought no attention whatsoever, which made a change.

Edmun, the king's messenger ushered the group into the palace via a set of narrow back streets and occasionally a tunnel or two, but soon they were immerging from a set of spiral stairs that lead up to a room where there was a roaring open fire and a table set for a king, in fact there was even a king, King Hamund Arnbjorg was sat in his favour red leather chair, one that had a high back and high enough arm rests so that he looked like he was nestled in all the luxury the palace could offer.

The king stood up and clicked his heels together on the arrival of his guests before bowing to each in turn and offering his hand for them to kiss, the king in turn took hold of Ingrid's hand and kissed it, then he did the same to Halla, Aatu just got another stern look.

The guests were told to sit and eat before any other business was to be discussed, the meals just kept coming and

Rogan for one was finding himself continually thanking the servants but turning them away. After about an hour, the king began to speak, first by asking about the journey, and then about the situation as far as they knew, and he said candidly that if his wife was involved in any way that she was not above the law.

"So, you think my wife is hiring these half-breeds, bloods or whatever they are, no offense intended, an army of mercenary creatures, she has about five hundred here alone and many more scattered about the kingdom, mostly in the cities and towns, not so much the villages, but why? For what purpose do they fulfil? Not to mention it must be costing her an absolute fortune?"

"We believe that she is planning to seize the throne for herself, and then after that perhaps to march on other sovereign states, who knows, but these Black Guard are not being paid just to stand on guard all day, are they?" stated the captain.

"However, it is not illegal just to hire guards to have them stand around and do nothing at all!" put in the king. "So, what evidence do we have that my dearly beloved has even broken so much as a fingernail, never mind the law?"

"We do have a witness to something else that has occurred in the palace, all be it over a couple of years ago now, but it might be the missing link between one thing and another."

"Captain Brecott, I asked for frankness now who is this witness and are they credible?"

"If we could just speak with Sister Wenyid Tanner, I think we might have our first piece of the puzzle."

"Did you that our dear sister is being put forward for sainthood, and she is still alive, have you ever heard anything like it before, but she will be at the cathedral will she not?"

"That I wouldn't know your excellency."

"Edmun, finish your drink and go find out, it is late in the afternoon now and I don't want our dear sainted sister brought here in her night attire, go, shoo!"

It was another hour before Edmun returned with Sister Wenyid. She was not at what Rogan or Ongar had expected, they might have imagined a rather older plumper women, more matronly type, perhaps, whose voice was gruff and stern, but to everyone surprise Sister Wenyid was lithe and wearing chainmail with a sword at her side, her hair was long and golden and her face was a picture of warmth and compassion.

Rogan was intrigued. "Forgive me, my lady, but is it true that you are called a saint?"

Wenyid threw her head back and laughed. "Don't believe everything you hear. I am but a pious sister married to the lord."

"Then he is a very lucky lord, sister!" Rogan said, drawing a hard stare from Ingrid.

"Come now sweet sister tell these noble gentlemen what you have really been up to, after all they have inquired after your credentials."

"Let me tell the story, please sister," implored the captain.

"You boys, honestly, go on then if you must but I had better get a sizeable donation to the church roof fund, if you are to bore me to death!"

Captain Brecott told how three years ago a fleet of Gnomes from Holsettia sailed across the Dark Water Channel,

212

the mighty river as wide as a continent, and landed in a country far to the south called, Faleacia and within weeks that mighty army of savages had swept across the country killing, looting. Raping and pillaging as they went, and no man nor army could stop them.

Sister Wenyid at the time was visiting one of their churches and it was attacked but she valiantly took up the sword of one of the fallen warriors and charged right into the marauding Gnome warband and single handedly killed them all.

"That's not true Ricsige and you know it, I killed but a handful and then the town militia found their second wind and they did most of the killing!" After that, Sister Wenyid and her militia friends chased the horrible little creatures right back to their boats and they sailed away with their tails between their legs.

"Wow!" That was all Rogan could muster.

Ingrid bowed her head in Wenyid's direction acknowledging her bravery and spirit.

"Now, if you have all finished with your over embellished stories, can I ask why I was summoned your majesty?"

"I need these gentlemen to hear your story of the confession of Æstrid Steinolf."

"Queen Helga dotes on the girl, Æstrid, and when she was thirteen years old, to mark the occasion, the queen threw a fancy-dress ball and hundreds of guests were invited, young Æstrid was newly a woman after her first bleed, and she was quite the beauty back then, well as the night wore on and people started to leave it was thought time for Æstrid to take to her bed chamber, here in this palace.

Now it was just a short while later that we all heard what a blood curdling scream was, and everyone ran upstairs to the sound that came from the girl's bed chamber, but only her mother, the queen and myself were allowed inside, there was no one else there at that time. Æstrid, said that she had been attacked by someone, someone she knew, when we asked who that someone was her mother and the queen were asked to leave the room, she wanted to make her confession before God and to me."

"Although the person that forced himself up on her was wearing one of those costumes and a mask, he let slip that the reason he was going to take her virginity was to teach her a lesson, he mentioned something that only her brother, Skuld could have known, not enough evidence to get him convicted by any magistrate at the time, and she was absolved publicly of any blame though she was worse for wear herself with fine wine, and I found out later from the church that the queen had paid a small fortune to buy witnesses to give Skuld an alibi."

"And now for the second damning piece of evidence, Sister."

"Well, this is harder to prove as the young servant girl who witnessed it has long since disappeared herself, fell off the face of the earth. Anyway, she was going about her duty in the queen's bed chambers when she heard what she thought was laughter and squealing and other matrimonial noises coming from the queen's bedroom, knowing that the king was away on business elsewhere she peered in through the crack in the door, and to her horror there was the queen in convulsions with Skuld, and both were naked as the day they were born and he was only fifteen himself at the time."

"This is almost too incredible to believe, and your highness I am so sorry that this account has been brought back to mind, shall we stop now and talk some more another time?" asked Rogan.

"No, please let our blessed sister continue, there is more."

"The next time the servant girl caught them together, she overheard the Skuld talking about if he were king, he would deliver all of the queen's enemies into her hands, and she quipped, what if everyone in the Shattered Realms were her enemy, what then, and Skuld boldly declared then he would build an army, take the Shattered Realms and give them for a foot stool to her feet."

"You say this girl disappeared, but did she have a name, maybe we can track her down, we have men in three different kingdoms as we speak."

"Solveig, she was twelve years old at the time I think."

"Solveig Arnulfrid? Wait a minute, she must be about fifteen or sixteen, yes?" Rogan asked Ongar.

"Yes, I suppose, I don't really know."

"How do you know the girls last name, have you seen her, or perhaps you met while captive to the orcs?" inquired sister Wenyid.

"She is one of my most trusted companions, my Gedriht."

"Then we can speak to her in person, Your Majesty you see this is the missing piece of the puzzle!" the captain said excitedly.

Just at that moment the double doors burst open and, in the doorway, illuminated by numerous torches in the corridor behind her stood the queen, and as her shadow flickered with the torch light the shadows accentuated her features and her standing, she looked both magnificent and terrifying at the same time.

"Oh, my darling husband, you are not having a party without inviting me, are you?"